Purrfectly Paired

A MAVERICK PRIDE TALE

C.D. GORRI

Copyright

Purrfectly Paired
A Maverick Pride Tale
by C.D. Gorri
Edited by BookNookNuts

Copyright 2022 C.D. Gorri

*To the amazing Readers, without you none of this would be possible.
Thank you for taking the time to read my stories.
Xoxo, C.D.*

Before you begin, sign up for my newsletter here:
https://www.cdgorri.com/newsletter

This story was previously published as Falcon's Heart.

Hello Readers!

Thank you for purchasing this Maverick Pride Tale featuring *Uncle Uzzi's Magical Matchmaking Service* and our favorite driver, Hank. I thought a lot about Hank's HEA ever since he first popped up in Purrfectly Mated, and I knew from the very beginning, this sexy Shifter was more than meets the eye.

I hope you enjoy his story.

Happy reading!
Xoxo,
C.D. Gorri

Blurb

Hank Garret doesn't need any help finding a mate. Too bad Uncle Uzzi won't take no for an answer.

Driving the infamous matchmaking Witch to visit the Maverick Pride is one of his favorite duties, but lately, it's the very thing disturbing the Falcon Shifter's peace of mind. Watching those Tigers find their true mates is just too painful.

When Uncle Uzzi recommends Hank's services to a Lioness in need, duty calls. It was fine. He could remain professional. He just has to ignore the gorgeous spitfire in his backseat for the next twenty-four hours.

Piece of cake–*gulp*.

Annabeth Golden of the Blue Valley Pride is one frustrated Lioness. Her family's reputation makes finding a mate hard, but is it really so bad? So, what if she *accidentally on purpose almost castrated* her high school boyfriend for being unfaithful? Was that cause to make her *persona non grata* with the entire Pride? Hard up for love and trying to win the big contest at work leaves Annabeth at her wit's end.

Good thing she runs into Uncle Uzzi of the infamous *Uncle Uzzi's Magical Matchmaking Service*. Annabeth has hit the jackpot–or so the she-Cat thinks.

But what happens when the cranky Falcon her Lioness pines for claims she's mistaken? Will this cat bag her bird?

Find out in this installation of the Maverick Pride Tales.

Preface

"What is this? Are you getting fancy on me now, Uzzi? I swear, Betty would have a field day teasing you," Richard grunted as he hefted the large package onto the kitchen counter.

"Ah, my liebling would love that I am taking care of my health, Richard. Come now, open," he instructed the ornery man.

"Look at all this. Perfectly portioned my foot. They must not know how you pack it away," he muttered loud enough for Uzzi to hear him.

Richard loved to complain, but since his beloved late wife had hired him to help take care of things for Uzzi while he worked, he could not see to getting rid of the man. Besides, Richard was a wonderful chef, and he was not wrong. Uzzi loved to eat.

"Fantastic," Uzzi enthused, despite his housekeeper's grumblings.

He waited impatiently for the other man to finish opening the package, clapping his hands in anticipation.

"*Eat Well Live Proud,*" Richard read the card aloud, handing it to Uzzi as he began removing the contents of the cooler box.

Uzzi wondered if the container was recyclable—probably considering who it came from. *Eat Well Live Proud* was the preeminent import/export company owned by the Blue Valley Lion Pride. To humans, they were just another internationally known business, famous for their farm to table services—a trend that was very popular these days.

Along with being a Witch and matchmaker extraordinaire, Uzzi was a foodie and loved to indulge his appetites with fresh, delicious, and sometimes healthy morsels. *Eat Well Live Proud* had just launched this smaller branch of their business, having only dealt with restaurants, hotels, cruise lines, and that sort of thing for years,

They mainly worked with ranches to deliver the best organically raised beef, pork, poultry, lamb and other meats like bison and ostrich, too. But Uzzi had heard wonderful things about their new conscientious and sustainable seafood line. He could not wait to sample it for himself.

"King Salmon? Hmm," Richard mumbled, and Uzzi saw the wheels working in the man's head.

"Yes, and some bass, too. And did you know they just signed a deal with some strictly organic, non-GMO farmers to deliver produce now?" Uzzi said.

"Uzzi, we live in the Garden State. Non-GMO organic produce is everywhere, for Pete's sake."

"Yes, well, still. This is certified by Lions, Richard. How could it be anything other than *wunderbar*?"

"So, will you be traveling this week? I am going to plan the menu now," Richard informed him as he put away the various packages of fish and meat in the freezer, taking two portions of salmon out to thaw for dinner.

Yum.

"Yes, I am planning to be here. But, Richard, take another piece of salmon out. We are having company tonight."

"Yes, boss."

Uzzi picked up his cell phone, his fingertips tingled with anticipation as he scrolled through his contacts. Something very important was happening in the universe, something leading him to this moment.

Part of Uzzi's talents lied in his ability to trust in the Fates to guide him. Right now, everything inside of him was screaming at him to make a call. His magic hummed and buzzed excitedly, blue sparks crackled at his fingertips.

Wonderful inventions, cellular phones, but they could be so temperamental. On and on, he perused the thousands of names saved inside the little gizmo. He'd met so many people over the years, helped scores of them to find their fated mates, too.

It was his burden and his gift, to bring together couples the universe had selected to be together. A worthy vocation, indeed. Suddenly, his magic heated, the buzzing grew louder, and then—zap!

Uzzi stopped scrolling and read the name of the contact that popped open on the small screen of his smart phone. Ah ha! He grinned widely.

Of course.

It was about damned time, too, in his not so humble opinion. Beneath the business, Falcon Limousine Service, was the name Hank Garrett. He was the owner of the car service, Uzzi's own trusted driver, and his honorary nephew.

The Shifter was the son of a man whom Uzzi had owed a favor to, once upon a time. Though he'd drifted from the parents, Hank had remained a favorite of his. The young Falcon had worked hard to build up his company, and Uzzi was proud to hire him whenever he needed.

Time and again, he'd offered his own services to the younger man, but Hank insisted he needed no help to find his mate.

Well, we shall see about that, dear boy.

"Hello, Hank? Yes, it's Uzzi. I wanted to invite you to dinner… Tonight… Yes. You're free, then? … How wonderful!"

Wunderbar, indeed.

Prologue

Annabeth gritted her teeth and waited impatiently for her boss to finish with the weekly meeting at the offices of *Eat Well Live Proud*.

The Blue Valley Lion Pride's corporation was responsible for procuring and delivering quality, organic, sustainably harvested, and eco-friendly meats and fish to restaurants, hotels, and just recently, private homes the world over.

With the launch of their new *EWLP Direct Line*, as in direct to your door, every Lion and Lioness in the company was working overtime. Not ideal for the thirty-something female who was days away from going into her heat cycle.

Speaking of heat, what the heck was the thermostat on, anyway? Annabeth was practically melting.

Pant. Purr. Gasp.

She rolled her eyes at her melodramatic Lioness. Her inner kitty could be a bit extra at times. Like now.

Grrrr.

Oh sure. Now she was pissed. Whatever. Annabeth flicked her gaze from one corner of the room to the other. She felt stifled in the crowded space. The walls were closing in on her.

How did no one else feel cramped? She bit back her sigh as Maggie Pierce, the big boss lady, rambled on about some convention she was sending some lucky—*ew, make that unlucky*—feline to represent EWLP. As if dressing up for another corporate bash was anyone's idea of a good time.

Who the hell wanted to go to another boondock town down the shore, anyway? Not Annabeth. Blue Valley was just under central Jersey, and she hated everything below it. At least here, she could still get to Manhattan once every couple of months for a Broadway show or to get some really delicious pizza, or dirty water dogs.

Grrrr.

Okay, so her inner kitty had a thing for questionable cuisine. She was surrounded by the good stuff 24/7. It was natural she'd crave junk food constantly, right?

Looking at her plus size curves, she frowned. Okay, fine, so maybe she should cut it out with the hot dog binge eating sessions in NYC so she could fit into one of her formal gowns and maybe go on trips like the one Maggie was talking about.

Whatever.

It didn't matter, anyway. She hated traveling. Especially flying. But she also did not do well driving long distances. Buses were too crowded for her Lioness. And trains were just unnatural.

Like, who was really driving those things, anyway? She'd never seen a conductor or train engineer in person. Just people who played them on children's TV shows. So yeah, travel by train? No thanks.

Traveling just wasn't her thing. No sane Lioness wanted to put her life in the hands of some over-caffeinated pilot or driver—who she wouldn't trust to make her a sandwich—to operate a couple of tons of heavy metal with her in tow.

Hard. Pass.

Hell to the no, her she-Cat agreed.

This Lioness was not leaving the safety of the hard ground beneath her feet or paws. She sighed, openly relieved when Cornelia's name came up in the conversation. That Lioness deserved to be stuck traveling to East Bubblefuck, New Jersey, for some boring ass conference.

She was a rude bitch who had it out for all the Golden sisters. But being the gracious female her mother raised her to be, Annabeth was sure their nemesis had some good qualities too.

Not, sniffed her inner pussy cat.

Okay, seriously though, if Cornelia was willing to run all over the world at the beck and call of Eat Well Live Proud—which is a heck of a lot more than Annabeth was willing to do—the female was okay in her book.

"Ms. Higgins," Maggie said to Cornelia, who was grinning like the stuck-up little brown noser she was, casting shade at the other people sitting there. Annabeth supposed she just could not help herself. Once a prat, always a prat.

"I want you to remain here. I have an assignment for you—"

"But Ms. Pierce, I'm already packed—" Cornelia began, practically choking on her shock.

Annabeth winced, embarrassed for the usually haughty little miss. How dreadful! She hated being the center of attention herself, but Annabeth could not even imagine being so publicly deflated.

Served her right for thinking she was better than all the others. The Blue Valley Pride was close knit as fuck. Almost everyone she'd grown up with worked for the company. In that way, EWLP was sort of an extension of high school—and every bit as awful from a social standpoint.

Ugh.

Her sister, Ariella, elbowed her in the ribs, and Annabeth turned her attention to Cornelia. Holy cow. The woman was completely losing her shit.

"This is the best thing I've seen in days," her sister whispered as Cornelia ran to Ms. Pierce and grabbed her arm with her claws almost extended.

"I *always* represent EWLP at the annual convention. I'm already packed. My dress was dry cleaned. I got my car detailed. Uh, everything is ready—"

"And yet, you aren't going," Ms. Pierce said with a slight growl in her voice. "In light of some recent contradictions in your quarterly reports, Ms. Higgins, you have been grounded. Your task this week is to perform an audit of all of your accounts."

The entire room gasped, shocked at the insinuation. If perfect Cornelia had to perform an audit, what would that mean for everyone else? Annabeth bit her lip. She would stand by her numbers, but this was truly worrisome. The entire Pride had a stake in the company. If things were not done properly, that could mean a lot of money for a lot of people.

"Well, that was not the way I wanted to announce this, but yes. Audits are happening this week. You will each receive an email with your tasks while this is going on. The company has decided to do small sections at a time, Cornelia just happened to be first. Now, I have made promises to the CEO, and the entire board, for that matter, and I will make sure that everything going on in this company is on the up and up. So, remember, while you are making your reports that I will be watching you."

"But about the convention—"

"It will go to someone else. Cornelia, I need you to meet with the liaison from the EWLP auditing team coming in from Florida today. They will start going over your accounts first."

"What? But why?" screeched Cornelia, clearly the female was not thrilled with her new assignment.

"Is there a problem, Ms. Higgins?" the boss lady asked.

"Um, no," she mumbled.

"Does anyone here have an issue with how I run things here?" MS. Pierce asked louder.

Every feline eye in the room is tuned and focused somewhere else. From windows, to dust motes, to lint on the carpet—gazes flicked around trying to find anywhere to land other than on the angry she-Cat.

Snort.

All eyes flicked to Annabeth. Uh oh. Did she just snort out loud?

"You are in trouble now," whispered Ariella unhelpfully.

"Ms. Golden?"

"No. Um. Present? Uh—I mean, *yes,* Ms. Pierce? Can I help you?"

Could you be more awkward?

No. Probably not, sighed her inner kitty.

Annabeth almost died when every eye in the room landed on her. She caught sight of the crimson tint coating Cornelia's overly made-up face and wondered if her own blush surpassed the skinny Lioness' blazing rage. Lord knew the woman was a couple of cards short of a full deck.

So, Cornelia got embarrassed by the big boss. Oh

well, it happened. And frankly, it served that haughty feline right, walking around like she was better than everyone else! Cornelia did not work any harder than the Golden girls did, but she snatched every opportunity to kiss their boss' furry butt.

She'd been that way since they were all cubs in the Pride's summer youth camp. Seriously. Always brown nosing the camp counselors. Cornelia was forever in everyone else's business.

She had a long history of being a two-face, and Annabeth was certain she was going to be the maker of her own demise. She'd gone after her own sister's mate at last year's tree lighting ceremony in the center of their Pride's gated community, like some shameless hussy, or so Annabeth's mother said.

Why, in twelfth grade, Cornelia had even let Annabeth's biggest crush, Tommy Furbanks, stick his fingers where good girls should never let bad boys touch—*unless they were going steady.*

Even worse, she'd found out the Lioness had only gone after Tommy after Cornelia had heard Annabeth's plan to ask him to prom. She'd been just crushed after that and had accepted Ronald Grunkel's hardly flattering prom-posal.

The Aardvark Shifter had sent Annabeth a box

full of live ants and a jar of chocolate sauce—*sooo gross*. But beggars and choosers and all that. At least she hadn't gone to prom alone like her sister Ariella.

Really, she should thank Cornelia for letting Tommy finger her before Annabeth could make an ass of herself by asking the dumb jock out. She was such a loyal creature, she'd likely have stayed with the creep, and she would be Mrs. Furbanks now.

Permanently stuck with Tommy, who'd incidentally turned into a real loser. After failing to land a pro-football contract, the Lion just let himself go. Dropped out of college, started eating nonstop, and was now a hundred pounds overweight and working as a janitor at their old alma mater.

Yay Blue Valley Lions—er, not.

Annabeth was certain he was trying to relive his high school glory days, but alas, time was fleeting. Annabeth should know. She'd gotten a tad rounder as the years passed herself. Not like Tommy, but still. Here she was on the cusp of middle age—okay, not quite, but close enough—thirty-three and not even one, single dating prospect and her heat cycle coming up like gangbusters.

In fact, none of the Goldens had any luck in love. Toni had come close, but she didn't like to talk about. Ariella seemed smitten with a certain sexy Dire Wolf, who happened to make the best dang steak Annabeth had ever tasted. And as for Adrianna, well, she was rather tight lipped about the whole thing. George, their baby brother, was just hopeless when it came to most things, including romance.

Hmm. He was a greedy, annoying cub. Always eating the last of our cereal. We could still end him, her inner animal suggested.

Okay, soooo sometimes her inner kitty was a homicidal maniac. It was another reason Annabeth ate her feelings. Stress eating was a way of dealing with the crazy kitty who wanted to hunt her own brother on one paw, and on the other, to pounce on handsome strangers to sniff to see if they were her mate.

Prrrr.

Yes, her beastie was looking for a Mr. Golden, but where was she supposed to find him? Annabeth already knew everyone in her Pride. There were no eligible Lion males left. Maybe she should be like Ariella and develop a crush on someone outside their circle. If only she were brave enough.

Sad rawr.

"Miss Golden? Annabeth, are you listening?" Ms.

Pierce repeated her name, and she jumped, turning her attention to her petite yet powerful boss.

"Sorry," she murmured.

The older Lionesses were known for their wily and fierce natures. Everyone knew the females of the Pride were the badasses, and Ms. Pierce had a reputation for cutting her foes down to size without even messing up her fur. Annabeth wanted to be her when she grew up.

"Yes, Ms. Pierce?"

"You will represent Eat Well Live Proud at the *New Jersey Convention for Quality Food Products* this year. You will need to be there in time for the ball on Friday night. I ordered a plane ticket—"

"But Ms. Pierce, I don't travel well," she blurted, astounded at her own bravery.

The older Lioness turned her golden gaze on Annabeth and took two steps forward. She felt everyone's stares on her but was too worried about her boss to look.

Good thing too, or she would've missed the telltale twitch on the corner of the she-Cat's mouth that usually spoke of extreme annoyance. Unfortunately, Annabeth had caused said tick a time or two in the past. It never ended well for her.

Gulp.

"It is hardly a long distance, Ms. Golden," Maggie growled. "I suggest you start driving now."

Annabeth swallowed and nodded. Ms. Pierce went over a few other points with their team, but Annabeth hadn't heard a word. She was too busy panicking.

Annabeth gathered her things shortly after they were dismissed, wondering how she was going to pull this off. Anxiety rushed through her veins and her stomach tightened. If only the absurd reaction could help turn her rolls into abs! Maybe then it wouldn't be just another annoyance.

Fuck. Fuck. FUCK.

Since when did Eat Well Live Proud send a plump little fluff of a Lioness Shifter to represent them? Hardly common practice. Cornelia looked the part, all sleek and sophisticated. Annabeth was her polar opposite. A bumbling sort of blonde mess. Her hair lacked the telltale color base most Lionesses had, somehow, she'd been born with a medium ash brown head of hair with only a few tawny streaks, whereas most of the Pride sported full on gold locks.

Odd duck, that's me.

She didn't have dark curls like her Ariella, or the pin straight mane Toni was born with. Nope. Annabeth looked more like a tired suburban housewife with her boring wavy ash brown with overgrown highlights—*natural, not from a bottle, fuck you very much.*

She wasn't all bad, of course. Sure, Annabeth was rounder than plenty of her peers, but she was a good Lioness, loyal to her Pride, dedicated to her family, and good at her job. She might not love her life, but she was happy enough. She had friends, men and women—though none were prospects for a mate. She had her sisters, her mother, and good working relationships with her coworkers.

Then there were her interests to keep her busy outside of work. She enjoyed reading, going to art shows, and listening to music—but Annabeth had a raunchy side too. She was fun-loving, too.

Her penchant for skinny dipping was not tempered at all by the fact her wide ass caused quite the splash whenever she cannonballed into whatever body of water she and her sisters frequented. They did that a lot in the warmer months, breaking into the community pool or the youth center for midnight swim parties.

It was all in good fun, and they hardly ever got caught. Mostly. The Goldens were infamous for their tomfoolery and sisterly shenanigans. George was usually too much of a goody-goody to join in.

But the Pride usually just blamed their outrageous behavior on their mother. Patricia Golden was one hootenanny of a mother and role model.

Because of that funny feline femme fatale's rearing, Annabeth, and her sisters alike, all spoke their mind, cursed like sailors, drank like fish, and lived their lives to the fullest, which typically meant gorging themselves on champagne, chocolate—*the sinfully rich kind*, and whatever else floated their boats.

Of all the Goldens, Annabeth was the only one who hated traveling, and spent way too much time crying over touching commercials—the ones with the kids spilling juice on the floor and splashing in it as they run away, making red footprints everywhere, but the perfect skinny mom comes in with a roll of paper towels her handsome hubby hands her and they both just sigh dreamily as she bends to clean the mess.

Sigh. Sniff.

Of course, if Annabeth was in charge of writing those commercials, the handsome hubby would clean the mess, pour his wife a cup of coffee, then kneel before her and massage her feet before flashing her a wicked little grin that meant bedroom shenanigans were a-happening-soon.

Grrrr.

But that was not her job. Nope. Her job was to go represent the company at the food convention—and Annabeth was going to do her job to the best of her ability. Hell, she was proud Ms. Pierce had chosen her for it.

So, onward and upward, impending heat cycle or not, Annabeth was going on a picnic of a trip, and she was bringing—*hmmm, what was she bringing?*

Crap.

She had to pack! Annabeth didn't believe in doing things half-assed, and part of being prepared for this kind of—*gulp*—business trip meant having the right clothes for the job. What did one wear to a food services convention, anyway?

One thing was certain, Annabeth was not asking Cornelia for advice. That feline had taste right up her ass, which was exactly how short she wore her skirts. Annabeth didn't need any middle-aged, paunch-having weirdos slapping her butt like she was one of the female employees on Mad Men, for fuck's sake. If there was one thing cable TV had taught her, it was the 1960s were a fucked up time to be a woman in the working world.

No, thank you.

"Are you still hanging around here, Golden?" Ms. Pierce snapped, and Annabeth almost peed herself.

"I'm leaving right now to grab my luggage, Ms. Pierce. Bye-bye," she mumbled as she raced out the door.

Lucky for Annabeth, it was the 21st Century.

Chapter One

With her heart pounding, her nerves a complete wreck, and her brain a jumble of half-finished thoughts, Annabeth rushed around her desk gathering her purse and the light jacket she'd worn that day.

Mother Nature liked to mess with New Jerseyans during spring. It was like the mystic goddess was playing roulette with the weather. Sometimes it was beautiful, warm, sunny, and just lovely. Often it was cold, windy, rainy, and downright miserable. The thing was, that all happened in the course of one day.

"Whatever," she mumbled to herself, swapping her work heels for a pair of neon pink crocs.

Comfort whenever she could, that was Annabeth's motto. Also, probably why she'd never been picked for this gig before. She'd only recently started wearing appropriate footwear inside the office because Toni suggested it.

She hated what she called Annabeth's orthopedic nurse shoes, but Annabeth did not give a fuck. Crocs were fucking awesome, and she had a dozen pairs in all colors and prints.

Okay, focus.

Annabeth unplugged her laptop and shoved it in her briefcase, then loaded up all her bags, only turning back to grab her cell phone. This was the first time Ms. Pierce had trusted her to represent *EWLP* at a convention, or anywhere, for that matter. Usually, the company only sent top salespeople, or important board members—you know, the kind of employees who were hell bent on climbing the corporate ladder.

As in, literally anyone else.

Annabeth was just not like that. None of the Goldens were. Maybe Toni, but that was only because she was some kind of numbers genius. Adrianna, Ariella, and Annabeth were far too easily distracted to get anywhere career wise.

This was her chance to do big things and change the Pride's opinion of her and her sisters. Maybe save their family name, or at the very least polish it up a little.

Holy moly.

The pressure just got real. Annabeth tried to steady her breathing, but she was about halfway to a panic attack. She could not fuck this up.

She had to go home, pack, take out the kitchen trash, and make sure Adrianna had the spare key to bring in the mail otherwise Mrs. O'Reilly, her neighbor, tended to read it—nosy old bitty. Impromptu business trips were so dang inconvenient, and she had zero time to mess around.

"Annabeth, wanna grab a coffee before you go?" Ariella called after her.

But Annabeth was already taking off down the hall, shaking her head, she turned around to answer her sister.

"I have too many things to do, but I'll call you later," she was saying, and naturally, as she spun to grab hold of the exit door, she collided with a short, very well-dressed older man, sporting the cutest white beard she'd ever seen.

"*OhMyGawdImSoSorryLookOut!*" Annabeth screeched as they both tumbled to the ground.

"Whoopsie! Are you okay, my dear?" The meticulously groomed gentleman asked, righting himself last minute.

In fact, he hardly seemed ruffled by all the fracas. Meanwhile, Annabeth was sitting on her ass with everything she'd been holding covering the floor.

"Crash and bash Annabeth, that's me," she grumbled, trying to right her skirt over the unflattering beige granny panties she had on.

Oh well.

It was Thursday, for Pete's sake. She didn't have a hot date or anything. Annabeth was a comfort over style kinda gal and would continue to choose practical over pretty but painful any day of the week. Not that she was worried about what the nice old man thought of her panty situation.

"Oh my, you dropped your briefcase. Here, let me help," he said and started collecting her spilled papers.

"Thank you. I am so sorry. I would say I never do that, but I would be lying," she only half-joked.

"I'm sorry you probably have to be somewhere. I got this," she began, but the older man glanced around, his blue eyes sparkling, then he touched his nose and something amazing happened.

Annabeth's papers began to shake and shimmy, and in the bat of an eye, they went from being sprawled everywhere, to being in a neat little pile in her hands.

"There you go," he said, and seemed very pleased with himself.

Annabeth's inner Lioness chuffed. She was alert, but did not sense any threat.

Witch, she whispered into Annabeth's brain, and being the smooth Shifter that she was, naturally, she blurted it out.

"You're a Witch, aren't you?"

"Yes, I am. Come, let's go outside a moment so I can see you are alright," the kind man insisted. "Oh, here," he said, bending down to retrieve the clear organizer bag she kept inside her purse.

The plastic crinkled in his hand. Annabeth froze, mortification rising. Of course, the bag was translucent and revealed an assortment of pads, tampons, lip gloss, and condoms —a whole bunch of them and all were more than likely past the expiration date.

"OMG! Kill me now," she mumbled. "Look, I am so sorry—"

"That's okay, dear. Best you be prepared for life's adventures, eh? My Betty would approve," the elderly Witch said, and his blue eyes sparkled with affection.

"Betty?"

"Yes. She was my wife for a very long time, and I miss her terribly. But I talk to her every day, don't I liebling," he said to the side.

"That is super sweet," Annabeth gushed.

"Thank you, dear. Come, we can sit on this bench here and you can tell me where you were going, taking off like a rocket!"

"Oh! I am so embarrassed," she replied, and giggled. "I'm sorry, Mr.?"

"Call me Uncle Uzzi," he replied with a twinkle in his eye and took her briefcase from her overflowing hands.

"You know, I don't know you from Adam, but I feel like I can trust you," Annabeth said.

Clearly, she bumped her head on the way down or something. Since when did she trust total strangers?

"You can trust me, Annabeth, I am great with secrets. Now, why don't you tell me what is going on?"

"Did I tell you my name?" she wondered aloud, but Uncle Uzzi just grinned and waited for her to continue speaking.

"Oh well, I suppose I did. Anyway, the thing is I hate traveling, you know? Flying makes me nauseated. Trains, no way. And I would drive, but I just have zero sense of direction and, well, I get distracted by shiny things," she mumbled and shrugged.

Annabeth was a lot of things and honest was one of them. She was not down on herself. Hell no. She loved her faults, took them in stride, and anyone who didn't appreciate them could just keep on moving. But this trip, ugh, this trip, had her stomach butterflies buzzing around like fighter jets.

She felt weird. Like she was on the cusp of something big. She turned to Uncle Uzzi, trusting the strange Witch for some reason, and waited for him to say something. The older man smiled gently, blue eyes sparking with magic and maybe a hint of mischief as he patted her hand.

"It's okay, Annabeth. Lots of people dislike traveling," the male Witch said.

His agreement made her feel oodles better. So much so that Annabeth continued her tirade to the total and complete stranger. Uncle Uzzi nodded sympathetically his sapphire stare full of understanding.

"I know it is silly but what kind of woman wants

to be completely at the mercy of someone else? Planes shouldn't even be capable of flight! And who trusts trains? We don't even see who drives them, for Pete's sake. Is it an engineer or a conductor, and aren't those words we use for other jobs?"

Okay, she was getting hysterical now. But there was just no stopping it.

"For all we know, every time we get on public transportation, we could be trusting our lives to some self-driving contraption. Like everything is really just a giant drone or something with a twelve-year-old kid operating it using an Xbox from home!" Annabeth shouted.

"Oh my, I never thought of it like that," the older man said with a wry grin, but that did not stop Annabeth from continuing her tirade.

"And you know what else?" she dropped to a mock-whisper, as she started going through the things she and Uzzi had collected from the ground, shoving them in the appropriate bags.

"What's that, dear?"

"You're a Witch, so I can say this without judgement. I'm a Lioness, right? Well, one of the biggest banes of my existence is having a freaking heat cycle. Oh yeah, you know what I mean. Propagation of the species and all that fun crap," she mumbled.

"Yes, I am aware of heat cycles. Can't you use something to stop it?"

"Been doing that since I was eighteen, but being a Shifter, my genetics make it impossible for any potion or medicine to work very long. Eventually, they become ineffective."

"I understand. That must be difficult," Uzzi sympathized.

"Oh yeah. And now my boss is sending me on this trip on the very weekend my heat cycle is due to start. Literally, any day now."

"What is the trip?" he asked.

"It's the *New Jersey Convention for Quality Food Products*," she told him, and shook her head.

"I see, and is there no boyfriend who will travel with you to this event?"

"What? Who me? No! No boyfriend," she replied and shook her head in denial.

"Annabeth, have you talked to your boss?"

"No! I can't refuse this trip. This is my chance to finally show my boss I can handle this kind of thing. But really, can you imagine being n a hotel full of horny, and probably married, creeps, looking for a little side bae action, and going into your heat? Happened to my cousin when she was on an assignment with her best friend's mate, and boy, was shit awkward after that weekend!"

"I see," the man said, reaching into his coat for his cell phone. "What's your address, Annabeth?"

"Oh, 645 Willow Avenue," she told him, and stared wide eyed. "Oh my, you must think I am insane! I am so sorry for basically kidnapping you, and dragging you outside, and making you listen to my nutty rant—"

Annabeth gasped. She slapped a hand over her mouth.

Crap.

She'd just had a full-blown panic attack and in front of a complete stranger.

"Not at all," the stranger smiled. "Now, I told you to call me Uncle Uzzi, but let me formally introduce myself. I am Uzzi Stregovich of Uncle Uzzi's Magical Matchmaking Service."

"Oh my Gods! You're famous," she gasped.

"Ha ha. Well, it is nice to be recognized, Annabeth Golden. But come now, listen, I think I have a solution to at least one of your problems."

"You do?"

"I believe so, sweet Annabeth."

"You know, I've heard of you a lot lately," Annabeth told him, cutting him off. "You're like the rock star of matchmakers!"

Uncle Uzzi smiled widely, then laughed at the apt description. He leaned forward, and Annabeth did the same, meeting his sapphire stare with her own clear, amber-hued gaze.

"You mentioned the inconvenient timing of your heat cycle and having no boyfriend. Now, I know of a Witch and a scientist who have teamed together to make custom elixirs for stopping said cycle, but that will take time. I am afraid it won't be ready for this weekend," he began.

"But that's amazing. If you have any information, I would be happy to reach out to them," she said, nodding.

"Indeed, I do. It is part of why I am here to meet with some members of your Pride. I am, of course, also here to offer my services as a matchmaker for those interested. Now for another, rather personal question," he began. "Do you like sex, Annabeth?"

"Sex?" she squeaked. Annabeth felt her cheeks burning. This was so embarrassing. The man was like a sweet grandfather figure, but here he was, talking about nookie and darn it, how was she supposed to reply?

"Y-yes," she said awkwardly. "I mean, yes. I can

talk about this. I am an adult. Anyway, what's not to like?"

The Lioness blushed, and nodded, convinced he wasn't getting fresh with her. Not this sweet old man.

"Good. And love?"

"Oh, um, sure, I think it exists, but I've never actually been in love, Uncle Uzzi."

"Never?"

"No," she said, and shook her head ruefully. Annabeth looked down at herself and sighed.

"Most men I date think I should be grateful that they even notice me. I get propositioned, but no one has ever made a declaration of love to me before. I doubt it will ever happen to someone like me."

"And just why not? What is wrong with you?"

"Mr. Stregovich—"

"What did I say? Call me Uncle Uzzi, please," he said, offering a kind smile. Annabeth blushed again and nodded, tucking her hair behind her ears.

"Okay, I'll explain," she said, more for herself than for him. "I'm a Golden. My sisters and I have a reputation in this pride, and well, a lot of the males —okay, all of them—steer clear when it comes to us."

"Why is that?"

"Welllll," she began. Oh, how to explain? "Uncle

Uzzi, my sisters and I have been known to play pranks, get in trouble, and did I mention that whole phrase there is no fury like a woman scorned thing is literally about us?"

"You all sound positively delightful," he said with a grin.

"Well, thank you, I think, but no Lion male feels that way. Especially not any Lion in the Blue Valley Pride, I can assure you. Also, there are the obvious reasons I am still single. I mean, duh," she said, looking down at herself.

"What reasons? You will have to explain."

"Oh, come on. Fine, I will say it, but understand I totally love my body. It's just, well, men want the unattainable and I'm not exactly a model here. I have thick thighs, no gap, except for the label on some of my jeans at home. Also, I have a huge appetite, Uncle Uzzi. I eat. And I mean, I eat actual food. Last date I went on, the guy demanded I pay for it since I ordered more food than he did."

That had been one helluva night, and Annabeth's pride still hurt a little. The guy had been a Shifter too. You'd think he would've been used to a woman who could pack away three orders of wings with no problem.

Sigh.

"Sounds like you've been dating the wrong men, Annabeth. Now, I know exactly what you need, but first, let's solve your traveling problems," the male Witch said and nodded.

"Alright, I suppose. But forgive me if I am not exactly hopeful."

"Nonsense. First, you do not have to beg forgiveness. Second, there is always hope, little one. Now, I assume you have no problem being around Shifters since you are a Lioness?"

"Of course not. Are we talking about mates? Cause I always imagined I would mate with a big, sexy Lion. But the Golden reputation has been a major cockblocker, *er*, pussyblocker?" Annabeth whispered, wondering which word was correct.

"I think *pussyblocker* might be apt considering you are feline," Uncle Uzzi replied with a grin. "Now, tell me more about your family while I send this message."

"Well, my mother, Patricia, is, well, let's just say she has a certain image most people run from. Rumor is she is dating someone, but she won't tell any of us who."

"Ah yes, I know her well. I am actually supposed to have lunch with her later today," Uncle Uzzi confessed.

"With Mom? Why? Is she looking for a mate?"

"Don't you worry about that, dear. You said you'd dreamed of mating a Lion, but are you open to other Shifters as well?"

"I mean, I guess so, but I don't want anyone who would change me."

"How do you mean?"

"I mean, most Shifter females I run into are svelte and muscular. My sister Toni has a body like a goddess. But not me. My sister, Adrianna, spent three years in a miserable relationship trying to fit a man who would never accept her. I won't do that. I guess what I am saying is I won't mold myself into something new for a man," she stated, and shrugged.

"Good for you, Annabeth. And no real man will ever ask you to do that. Now, I see you, dear, and I have a pretty good idea what I am doing. DO you trust me?"

"Yes, surprisingly, I do," she said and cleared her throat. "You know, few women my age will say this out loud, but I am perfectly happy with myself. I don't want some meathead suggesting I start exercising or stop eating carbs—heaven forbid. And I don't want to pretend to like jazz or sculptures or whatever either."

"I would never set you up with a guy like that,

Annabeth," Uncle Uzzi said seriously. "What I am thinking is that you need someone to see you through your heat cycle, and you need a ride to the convention. Is that accurate?"

"Well, I suppose that is accurate. I would definitely be happy if I could see my heat through with someone who wasn't, you know, coerced or bribed by my mother."

The last time she'd had this discussion with her mother, Patricia Golden had advertised for a stud for her young daughter. Literally. Her ad read "seeking stud to sex up a fine feline—must be packing ten inches or more" and the bad news did not end there.

Humans got ahold of the supposedly Shifter-only newspaper, and they thought it was a cat breeding service.

Sad meow.

Annabeth still received phone calls to that effect. Humiliating? You bet. Especially since no one in the Pride had answered the ad. Her sisters had come to the rescue, telling everyone it was a gag. But it hurt then, and it hurt now.

"I see," Uncle Uzzi said. "What about finding your mate? Is that a priority?"

"I would love to find my mate," Annabeth

confessed in a low voice. "But I don't think I have one. Not everyone gets a fated mate, Uncle Uzzi, surely you see that in your line of work?"

"Quite the contrary, love," Uncle Uzzi replied kindly. "Let's talk pragmatics. Just tell me about the kind of man you are looking for to spend your heat with. I don't want you to worry about a thing."

Annabeth's eyes took on a dreamy glow as she summoned the image of her fated mate in her mind. Detailed lists she'd outlined from the time she was a cub appeared in her eidetic brain.

"Okay, so I will go with my vanity list first. I want a man who is good looking—*obviously*. I am as much a fan of muscles and a handsome face as the next female. But I also prefer a man to have brains, a sense of humor, interests in things other than sports and scratching his own balls," she said, and Uncle Uzzi laughed.

"And should he be good in bed?"

"Yes," Annabeth confirmed, and felt her face positively flame. "I am not a virgin, but I've found sex to be seriously lacking since college. If a man could make me burn for him, like do the job so I didn't have to finish myself after, hell, I would be incredibly surprised."

"How do you mean?"

"Guys my age usually expect the woman to do it all," she blurted. "I mean, what the hell? Put in a little effort, for fuck's sake," she said and covered her mouth with her hands. "Sorry, I have a terrible potty mouth sometimes."

Uncle Uzzi took her hand and squeezed it, laughing out loud. The older man shook his head and wiped his eyes, shooting a text off before looking back at Annabeth.

"Sorry about that. My dear, may I say I can tell you are going to be a delightful handful, Annabeth Golden. And I think I have just the man for you."

Annabeth stared wide-eyed at Uncle Uzzi and swallowed before nodding her head.

"Okay. I'm game."

"Good," replied the Witch, his blue eyes sparkling with magic. "Very good."

Chapter Two

"Listen up everyone, today *Falcon Limousine Service* is proud to announce the opening of our ninth new base of operations on the East Coast," Hank Garret announced to the room of drivers currently lounging in the break room. "*Falcon Limousine Service Station Nine* is officially a go."

He turned to look at his crew, rolling his eyes at the smattering of applause. Fuckers. They were usually a little more enthusiastic about things like this. Especially, ever since he'd given the drivers who had been with him longer than five years stock options.

Then again, the mood around *Falcon Limousine Service Station One*, located in Manhattan, had been a bit melancholy ever since Antonio was dumped by his ex. The Cougar Shifter had been so distraught, he'd packed his shit and left a note saying he was done. Last Hank had heard, he'd gone back home to West Virginia somewhere.

Poor guy.

"Oh shit, really? That the one by Maccon City, boss?" Carter, a Lion Shifter from Blue Valley, jogged Hank from his reverie with his enthusiasm.

The man was the size of a bus. Literally. Hank could see why as he watched him slap together a triple decker peanut butter and strawberry jelly sandwich.

Fucking Lions.

Hank's Gyrfalcon bristled. The feline Shifters were always large, not to mention nutty. Not that he was lacking in the size category. Hank was tall and muscular as they come and not without good reason.

His inner beastie was the largest breed of falcon found in nature, and since Shifters often outweighed their wild cousins in animal form, it stood to reason they did in human form as well.

He was as muscular as the feline, but that was as far as the comparison went. Lions, especially the ones from Carter's Pride, were a handful. As a rule, he steered away from the rascally furballs. Especially when it came to dating them.

"So," Carter interrupted his musing, taking a monstrous bite. "Company's really making it then, huh, boss?"

Strawberry jelly dripped out the corner of his mouth and the Lion winked, giving Hank a lopsided grin. The Falcon inside of him closed his eyes, wishing like hell he could unsee the half-masticated sandwich the feline was currently chomping on.

"Yes, Carter. The company is solid."

Hank had a thing about sloppy eaters. As in, he couldn't bear to look at them. The raptor half of his dual nature agreed with a shake of his deadly beak.

Sigh.

The Lion kept on chomping without wiping his mouth. Hank almost lost it, but he was rescued from having to strangle his employee and figuring out how to dispose of the body by Henrietta. Apparently, Hank wasn't the only one who had issues with watching the messy Lion eat.

"How can you do that?" Henrietta, a Rabbit Shifter, shook her head at the admittedly absurd amount of strawberry jelly on the man's sandwich, and more importantly, on the front of his shirt. Slob.

The female growled and grabbed a paper towel from the roll, wiping it hard across Carter's face.

"Ow! Fuck, Hen, you took off my freaking skin with that!" Carter growled, shoving another enormous portion in his mouth and swallowing it down in one bite.

"Dude!" Hank shook his head at the man and tossed him the rest of the roll.

"Thanks, boss," Carter replied and winked.

Hank rolled his eyes, wondering if he didn't do it on purpose just to rile him. Of course he did. Fucking pussy.

"Change your shirt before you head out. And to answer your other question, yes, it's the Maccon City station. The ten cars I sent arrived, and I will be conducting interviews today for a manager."

"That's real good news, boss!"

Carter smiled again and Hank's eyes widened. The Lion's smile was a thing of pure horror, considering he had just shoved the other half of his sandwich in his mouth. A gory mess of peanut butter and red goo. Like some B-horror film meant to torture rather than terrify.

Yuck.

"I thought cats were neat," Henrietta said and made gagging noises. Hank just frowned.

"Only when we eat," Carter said, waggling his eyebrows.

"You're kidding, right?" the Rabbit Shifter flicked her hair over her shoulder and turned her nose up at the feline's antics.

"You know, I might visit the new station sometime soon, if I can get the time off. Maybe apply for manager," the Lion said.

"Oh, yeah?"

"Hell yeah! We're a family, man. Anything I can do to help, you know that."

"Okay then. I'll look for your application," Hank replied and nodded.

It was touching the Lion thought of their little car company as family. Hank was not so sure he was management material, but he could be wrong.

Family.

The word stuck in his head like a neon sign. Hank's father had some very particular ideas about what constituted family. Such as species and genus.

Maybe he was bigoted, but Hank's father was a good man. Right? Hank cupped a hand over the back of his head and exhaled sharply. He'd recently discovered a breathing regime designed to help ease his anxieties, and he could not deny, his father was a major fucking source of angst.

He'd been pissed when Hank had decided to open a business—and not just any business, but a driving service. Of all the things for a flight Shifter to be into, cars were something his old man just didn't understand.

It shouldn't matter what his father thought of his company, but he could not help but feel he let him down. Sure, Hank loved what he did. But he missed his parents. He still wished he could have made them proud when they were alive.

His Gyrfalcon stirred, and Hank took a moment to settle the beast. His inner bird always wanted to Shift when he thought about his parents. Their relationship had been difficult, but Hank tried to be a good son.

Maps had always fascinated him as a kid, and he'd spent countless hours making up routes to get from one place to another. Now, Falcon Limousine used sophisticated software courtesy of *Graves Enterprises,* protected by the highest security firewalls by *Draco Fortis,* in order to get his clients the fastest, safest, and most discreet luxury rides of their lives.

"Okay, let's get to work," he grumbled when he noticed everyone still standing there.

Hank clapped his hands loudly, and everyone got

moving, including Carter, who whipped off his shirt before leaving the room. Hopefully, to change into a clean one.

"Holy cow," whispered Henrietta as he exited the room.

Her gaze flashed to her boss and her cheeks heated at being caught ogling the man. Hank was so not getting into that conversation, so he just nodded at her to move it.

Fucking Lions.

Carter failed to note the effect his shirtless state had on the females who worked with him. Hank wished he was just as oblivious, unfortunately, he was not. But because he was a good boss, and a smart man, he ignored it.

Possible office romances aside, Carter and Hen, and the rest of his crew, for that matter, were excellent drivers and loyal to boot. He would not have hired them otherwise. Those two had been with Hank since the beginning. They owned a share of the corporation and worked harder than anyone else he knew.

When asked to head their own stations, both refused, citing almost exactly the same reason. They'd rather work with him, and the city didn't need two *Falcon Limousine Service* stations. Carter's interest in the new Maccon City station was an interesting development.

"Okay, everyone, your itineraries will hit your tablets any second now. Back to work, and be safe out there," Hank said, walking back to his office.

Though he was the CEO and owned the most stock in *Falcon Limousine Service*, he still drove as often as he could. Yes, he was ultimately responsible for the corporation, the marketing, development, finance, and human resource decisions, but he was most at home behind the wheel of his custom enhanced Rolls Royce Phantom limousine.

While he waited for his laptop to boot, Hank grabbed his work tablet. A familiar zing grabbed his attention, and he grinned. Looked like his Uncle Uzzi was back in the tri-state area. Hank smiled to himself as he read the older Witch's email.

He could just imagine what mischief the white-haired matchmaker was up to. His honorary uncle, Uzzi, was a friend to both his parents before they'd passed from a rare disease that affected bird Shifters.

He'd been a solid figure in his teen years and later. Hank made sure to always be on call whenever Uncle Uzzi needed him. No one knew him as long or as well as the old Witch.

The strands of gray threaded throughout Hank's

hair were a testament to that. His just reward for causing Uncle Uzzi to have more than one heart palpation when he'd been growing up, or so the man had always said. Hank was something of a daredevil in his fledgling days. At any rate, he loved the old man and was looking forward to seeing him again. As long as Uncle Uzzi didn't try any funny business.

Uncle Uzzi's Magical Matchmaking Service might be the reason the Witch was renowned throughout the entire world—*and beyond*—but Hank did not need his services.

Nope. Period. End of discussion.

When Hank was ready to settle down, he would do so without the famous matchmaker. He could find his own mate in his own time. The female he envisioned would be a lovely Falconess. One who was prepared to be a loyal wife and devoted mother.

His perfect mate would be serene and calm. A real lady who would not complain about his need to be on the road now and then. Driving was one of his passions, just like flying. He looked forward to the day he would be a mate and father, sharing his passions with his family. His inner raptor stirred with thoughts of his own young and a woman to fill the void inside of him.

Hmmm. Maybe it was time, after all. But a match-making service? Nah.

Even a famous one run by his incorrigible, yet delightful, and beloved Uncle Uzzi was completely unnecessary.

Hank had another reason for waiting on the whole *find a mate* thing. His parents were both Gyrfalcon Shifters, and immensely proud of that fact. One of the rarest species in the Shifter world, his mother and especially his father had impressed upon him the responsibility he had to continue their bloodline.

"Our kind is rare and special, Hank. It is your duty to see us flourish."

Hank's father had been a stern, severe sort of man. He told his only son the same thing from the time he was a fledgling. Hank knew it was old-fashioned, and maybe even a bit prejudiced. But he had made a promise, and his own innate sense of duty forced him to honor their wishes.

No matter what he wanted in life, he was obligated to continue the line. When Hank took a mate, she would be a female Gyrfalcon Shifter.

So, no, he would not need to bother Uncle Uzzi for his services. Hank did not need the old man's help to find him one of those. He had it all worked out.

The *North American Tower*, that was the official term for a group of Falcons, spanned the entire continent. With only a few hundred *Gyrfalcon* members, all he had to do was contact the registry and they would pair him up with an eligible female in no time.

Hank had already sent them his resume a few months back. He was waiting patiently for their office to contact him with possible matches. Of course, they had to do the standard tests to make sure he was not even remotely related to any of the eligible females. Something that caused him endless anxiety whenever he thought about it.

Breathe in and out.

Then there were the regular hangups. Agreeing to meet a stranger with the intention of essentially tying yourself to her for life was scary as fuck. Like what if she was boring, annoying, or hated him on sight? What if she smelled funny or made noises when she ate?

Hank's stomach tensed as he imagined agreeing to mate a total stranger, but it was what it was. He couldn't imagine Uncle Uzzi wanting him to mate for anything other than love, but surely, the man understood honor. Hank made a promise. He just had to see it through. There was no other choice.

Sighing heavily, he replied to Uncle Uzzi's emailed invitation with a firm no. Not surprised at all when his cell phone chimed a moment later. Hank turned it off. Not in the mood for the tongue-lashing he was sure to give him. Turning to his computer, he lost himself in missives until the door to his office slammed open.

Uh oh.

In all his musings, Hank forgot one thing about his world-famous uncle. He never called unless he was close by.

Gulp.

His inner raptor shivered and ducked his head. Uncle Uzzi had the uncanny ability to make him feel like a kid caught with his hand in the cookie jar.

Fucking hell.

And yet he loved the man.

Sigh.

Hank turned to face Uzzi with a chagrined smile on his face, hoping to smooth his ruffled feathers. He was not a rude person by nature, and he regretted his treatment of the elderly Witch immediately.

"So, you are available after all, nephew mine?"

"Uncle Uzzi!"

Hank opened his arms to embrace the older man in a big, back-slapping hug. Uzzi's blue eyes glittered at him like sapphires in the dingy space, and he winced as a zap of the man's magic stung him on his butt.

"Ouch!"

"Hmm, you've annoyed me, boy," Uzzi told him zapping him with his magic one more time, before clapping Hank affectionately on the shoulder.

The old Witch never stayed mad for long. Thank fuck. Hank's ass couldn't take much more getting zapped. He gazed around his dusty office and frowned. Hank really needed to hire a maid, he thought distractedly.

"So, Uncle Uzzi, what brings you in?"

Hank tried for nonchalance, but one look at his expression and he knew he should have armed himself. The unbelievably girl-like screech that emanated from Hank's lips one micro-second after his usually jovial Uncle Uzzi grabbed his right earlobe, flicking the thing with his blunt fingernails, would have been embarrassing if the office wasn't already soundproofed.

Fuck!

The man was fierce as fuck when he wanted to be. A lesson Hank had learned repeatedly over the years. But he also gave a damn about him, which was more than he could say for almost every other adult in his life.

"Don't you *hello* me, you birdbrain!"

"Come on, Uncle Uzzi. Not this again," Hank mumbled and pulled out a chair for the old man, rubbing his own ear as he waited until he sat down.

Uzzi always looked so smartly dressed. He had a style all his own, usually wearing white to match his hair and beard, sometimes with accents in primary colors. Today, he wore a silk ascot the same blue as his eyes. It would have looked crazy on anyone else, but Uzzi simply looked charming.

"It is really good to see you," Hank said, smiling genuinely at Uzzi.

The man was the closest thing he had to actual family these days. He hated disappointing him. Hank's heart warmed when, after a tension filled moment, Uzzi returned the look.

"And it is good to see you too, my boy," Uzzi said, clasping his hand before he remembered he was pissed at Hank.

Grumbling under his breath, Uzzi flicked his finger in the air and a bolt of blue magic whizzed past Hank's face and zapped him in his earlobe this time. Like a magical ear flick.

"Ouch!"

"What the hell are you thinking? Letting those feather-faced idiots find you a mate when you know perfectly well that is not how this works, Hank!"

"Fuck. How did you find out?"

"I have my ways. Surprising you even have to ask, my featherheaded friend," Uzzi growled and frowned, squinting at him as if trying to read his mind.

Dammit.

He was a wonderful uncle, but scary too. The Witch had the uncanny ability to tell when Hank was full of shit. And as far as Hank knew, Uzzi was never wrong about mates. Sure, the old Witch believed in fated mates, but Hank was not so sure that was for everyone. And if he did, well, who was to say this was not his fate?

"I knew you were a feather head! The North American Tower can hang itself, Hank. They won't know what you need—"

"It is always nice to see you, Uncle Uzzi, but the Tower has already been contacted," Hank interrupted, ignoring his tirade of bird-related insults. He'd heard them all, already.

"Hank, you know I just want the best for you," Uzzi began.

"I know, Uncle Uzzi, but I made a promise to my parents," he said, finally filling the old man in on the real reason for his decision.

"What?" Uzzi stilled, his eyes wide as he waited for Hank's explanation.

"You know what father was like. I disappointed him in so many ways, but before they passed, I promised him I would mate a Gyrfalcon to secure our place in this ever-changing world. We're too rare for me to just forego my duties. I can't let him down, Uzzi."

"Oh, Hank. Okay, I understand," the old Witch whispered, deflated. "And you don't care that the Fates might have another path for you?"

"I don't know if I believe in all that," Hank told him honestly, rubbing a hand over his face.

"Alright, Hank," Uzzi said, eyes narrowed. "I will leave this conversation alone, but I did not just come here for that. I need you to do me a favor."

"What's that?"

"This trip you are taking to see the Tower, it is soon, yes?"

"Yes. I have to be there this weekend for the final meeting in their interviewing process."

"I see, well, I have a client in need of a driver.

Would you be opposed to that? I believe it is on your way."

"A passenger?"

"Yes. I have the client's itinerary and final destination here," Uzzi said and withdrew an envelope from out of thin air.

Hank was still shocked whenever the old Witch did that. Magic was fascinating! But he would have to subdue his shock and awe, taking the packet from Uzzi intently.

"Alright, Uncle Uzzi. I will drive your friend to where he needs to go. As long as I get to the Tower by this weekend. They're meeting in South Jersey this year."

"Are they? Imagine that. That is exactly where this client needs to go. Well, good luck to you."

"Thank you, Uncle Uzzi. Hey, I'm still one of your favorite nephews, right?"

"You know you are, even though I find you infuriating. Now, walk me out, Hank," he said, embracing the younger man tightly.

"Love you too, Uncle Uzzi," Hank said easily, returning his hug as he walked him out the door.

Now, why did that feel too easy?

Hank had to admit, he expected the old man to put up more of a fight. He watched him get into the elevator, then walked back to his desk where he opened the envelope Uzzi had given him.

Hank checked over his client's schedule. He turned the page and froze, his blood boiling, he took in the snapshot of the pretty golden-eyed female staring up at him.

"No. No fucking way. He did it anyway, didn't he? Uncle Uzzi!" he roared, but the man was already gone.

His heart pounded inside his chest. His blood raced like thunder, crashing inside his head. He could hardly breathe as he took in the female's image. Then he dropped his eyes and read her name.

Annabeth Golden.

Even her name sounded fucking beautiful. Just like her. She was smiling at whoever had taken the picture with a twinkle in her eye, like they were sharing a private joke, and suddenly, Hank's curiosity turned green with envy.

Hell no.

He shook his head, refusing to get caught up in Uzzi's mischief. But his eyes refused to listen to reason. They dipped farther down the printed pages as if of their own accord, eager for every bit of information he could glean. Hank reread the little info passage and swallowed hard. Then, he reread it again. And that was when calm, sedate, unflappable Hank Garret really lost his fucking shit.

"Fucking sonovabitch!" he growled, slamming his hands on his desk.

Uncle Uzzi's new client was not just someone. She was a flippant, foolish, furry feline from the very same Pride as that thorn in his side, Carter! A flighty, flirtatious, completely infuriating little Lioness who, ironically, was not fond of travel.

"I won't do it," he growled, crumpling the paper in his hand, but even as he said it, he knew he would.

Sure, it seemed his uncle was up to his old tricks, but there was simply no way Hank was falling for it. He was an impeccable driver, playing the role of chauffeur to perfection whenever he escorted Uncle Uzzi around. He'd always preferred Uzzi's clients to think of him as a consummate professional—lest they try to hoist their sisters, daughters, or any other female relatives and acquaintances off on him.

Truth was, Hank Garret was not just a business owner and a rare Gyrfalcon Shifter. He was heir to the Garret fortune. Ever since he was a young man, whenever someone found out about his inherited wealth, they always had a female relative just dying to meet him. It had been that way throughout college and grad school until he dropped out of society.

Hiding the fact of his fortune, Hank opened his company, doing what he loved most. Uncle Uzzi supported him the entire time, and as of now, he was the only person who knew just how wealthy and influential the Garret family really was.

Of course, nowadays he put most of his money to work for others by funding medical clinics, soup kitchens, orphanages, free child aftercare facilities that offered tutoring, and shelters for abused women, and runaway teens. Something else his Uncle Uzzi had helped him with.

Hank did not mind working for a living. IN fact, he loved it. But no he did not have to work. He'd kept enough of the family funds for his future family, as well as the old homestead and some other properties.

Right now, *Falcon Limousine Service* meant everything to him. It was the perfect place for him to hire misplaced Shifters, offering them steady work and responsibility their animals needed, as well as the added benefit from being with others, even if their species were different.

Shifters needed community. He understood that

better than most. If only his Uncle Uzzi understood his need to honor his parents request he mate a Gyrfalcon to carry on the line, then everything would be fine.

Staring at the luscious image of his new client, Hank had half a mind to send someone else on the assignment. He had his cell phone out and was dialing Carter before he even knew what he was doing.

"Yeah, boss?"

"Carter, do you know an Annabeth Golden?"

"Golden? From the Blue Valley Pride. Fuck, boss, if that's who I think it is, turn down that job. That family is nuts!"

Hank growled into the phone. His Falcon was not happy at the way Carter carelessly spoke of the female. In fact, his bird was downright pissed.

"Boss?"

"Never mind, Carter," he clicked off the call.

It was fine. He would drive the woman. There was nothing to worry about. Hank was not interested in mating a feline. Hell, if Uncle Uzzi thought this Miss Golden was his mate, then perhaps the old Witch was losing his touch.

The memory of that last zap of magic Uzzi had given him made Hank's earlobe tingle. He rubbed it and changed his mind. Nope, Uzzi still had it. He was just mistaken about Hank.

Not nearly insulting, right? Hank's inner Gyrfalcon thought, slightly panicked at the idea of being zapped again.

Whatever.

Hank narrowed his cobalt blue eyes at the envelope before flipping through the papers inside. Never one to ignore responsibility, he made a promise to Uzzi, and he would keep it. Hank dialed the contact number and winced when a loud roar met his ears.

See? This is what happens when you deal with furballs, he thought unkindly.

"Whoops! My bad! That was my, *er*, cat," a decidedly sweet, feminine voice spoke up after the annoying snarl.

Hank seemed to forget his manners as his Gyrfalcon suddenly pushed forward with a growl of interest.

"Hello? Hello! Is someone there? Who is this?"

"Grrr," his Gyrfalcon's growl escaped his lips before he had a chance to recover.

Uh oh.

Almost as stunning as his beast's reaction was the

hard evidence of his arousal pulsing beneath his pants. Fucking hell, what was going on?

"This is Hank," he swallowed hard.

"Um, okay. Hi, Hank. What can I do you for?" the husky-sounding voice was laced with sleep, and maybe something else, as the speaker tried again to determine who he was.

"Are you asleep?"

"Well, that's kinda serial killer to ask, Hank. But since I'm more naïve than most, I'll give you another chance. Who or what are you?" she asked, yawning louder.

Better set her straight, his inner bird pressed harder.

Hank's chest was rumbling, his palms were sweating, and there was a loud roaring in his ears when he opened his mind to speak—only the words that came out of his mouth weren't what he'd planned on saying. His heart beat a rapid tattoo in his chest as his own voice echoed through the receiver.

"I'm yours."

Chapter Three

" *I 'm yours.*"

Annabeth sat up in her bed. When had she fallen asleep? Fuck! She was supposed to be packing! Panic filled her. What time was it? What the hell did it matter?

The sexy voice growling at her through the phone sent notes of arousal spiking through her still sleepy blood. Annabeth closed her eyes and cleared her throat.

"Um, excuse me," she mumbled. "Can you say that again?"

"Uh, I mean, I'm your driver," Mr. Sexy-Voice-Over-The-Phone corrected himself to Annabeth's utter disappointment.

"Oh," she said, wondering why her heart was beating double time.

"Um, okay," she added as realization dawned. "Did Uncle Uzzi make my travel arrangements with you?"

Annabeth stood up, probably too quickly, since her stomach lurched, and her head felt light. She took in the disheveled state of her apartment with a reluctant sigh. She would have to do a load of laundry if she were going to finish packing and be ready for the sexy sounding stranger to pick her up later that evening.

Sounds yummy, her Lioness chuffed.

Her inner kitty was so bad sometimes. Annabeth closed her eyes and pushed the overenthusiastic feline back down. Even with her impending heat that was no excuse for her to get frisky over a little phone call.

"Yes," the stranger answered, bringing her attention back to the conversation.

"Boy, you're really a chatty Cathy."

"Excuse me?" Mr. Sexy-But-Annoyed replied.

Sigh. It figures.

Dude sounded like a tight ass, and Annabeth was just riled up because of the naughty sex dream she'd been having from her catnap. Damn heat cycle was even invading her sleep.

"Nothing. Just one sec," she mumbled, and took a sip from the glass of water on her coffee table.

Dehydrated after the surprise brunch her mother had brought over to celebrate her upcoming trip, Annabeth had imbibed more than her fair share of icy cold mimosas and petite pastries and mini quiches. Parched, she wound up chugging all twenty ounces of the clear, cool liquid. Force of habit, she shrugged and dropped the empty glass back on the table with an audible sigh.

"Are you okay?" Grumpy-doodles asked.

"Hmm? Oh yeah, fine, sorry. What were you saying?"

She grabbed a piece of paper and listened to his tersely given instructions, wondering what had crawled up his butt and died. He had all the warmth of a glacier and the personality of a corpse.

Sheesh.

"Are you listening to me, Ms. Golden?"

"Yes. I got it. Be ready. Downstairs. You are on a time constraint. Yadda yadda. Fine. Yes. Got it."

"Fine. I will see you then."

"Fine," she rolled her eyes.

Ugh.

The movement proved too much, and she held her head against the sudden wave of dizziness that assailed her. Shifters did not usually get drunk or experience hangovers. However, when you were a Golden, you never could tell when something extra might make its way into your system.

Freaking Mom, she thought with a growl.

After Annabeth's chance meeting with Uncle Uzzi, she'd come home to find her mother waiting with a surprise feast. Toni and Adrianna had come home for lunch as well. And they'd had a mini going away party.

So, they'd started with mimosas, but switched to tequila and orange juice soon after. Of course, you couldn't have tequila without taking shots, and after a few dozen of those, plus whatever Mommy had slipped into her drinks, Annabeth had passed out midway through her packing.

Of course, as it always happened whenever her mother joined her and her sisters to celebrate, things got fuzzy once her eyes were fully opened. And also predictably, Annabeth woke up with less clothing than she'd started the day with.

Her frivolous feline mother had probably spiked everything from the croissant to the Cuervo. Annabeth growled. She did not have time for this crap.

Still, there was a bright side. Small, but bright, nonetheless. At least Annabeth did not detect the slight nausea that came the morning after she had been unknowingly *catnipped* by her own mother.

Last time that happened, she and her sisters went midnight skinny dipping in the creek just beyond the Pride's woods. Antonette had gone in with her, and if she recalled correctly, maybe one or two of their new Dire Wolf neighbors, and a few other Shifters who'd been hanging out at their roadhouse, had been there.

Talk about a night! But that was only after her mother had totally embarrassed Annabeth by telling everyone who had ears that her daughter needed a few rounds with a thick dicked Shifter before her heat cycle came upon her this year.

Fucking hell. But Patricia Golden was a woman on a mission. The Lioness wanted grandcubs sometime this year, and apparently, she did not care how she got them. Would even stoop to propositioning men for her daughter.

Sigh. Mothers.

It was like getting one of her kids knocked up was suddenly a priority for Patricia. Same with every other older Lioness in the Blue Valley Pride. They all wanted grandcubs.

Ever since Prince Leo announced he and his mate Sheila were expecting, the Pride's matriarchs had been harping on every eligible female to get mated and producing already. Unfortunately, the Golden sisters, and their brother George, had no prospects to speak of.

"So, what time will you be here again?" Annabeth asked once the guy with the dreamy voice finished going over all his rules for the drive.

"As soon as I can. Address?"

Annabeth rattled off the address to her condominium in Blue Valley and hung up the phone.

"I have to finish something first, but I will be there in one hour and fifty-three minutes."

"Not one hour and fifty-two?"

"No. I always observe the traffic laws, and as long as there are no surprises on the way, I will be there like I said, in one hour and fifty-three minutes."

"Oookayyy."

What a weirdo, she thought.

He'd hardly talked to her, and to be honest, the man seemed a little bit high-strung. This clearly could not be the guy Uncle Uzzi had promised would help her through her heat.

Annabeth wondered if she should call the old Witch with her mother's implicit instructions that the male who would help her through this cycle be hung like the infamous stud horse Galileo, whose exorbitant fees for siring champions were well-deserved—*just ask anyone in the horsing world.*

It didn't matter, anyway. Annabeth would not be creating any cubs this go round. Maybe not ever. She was simply one of those destined to be alone.

Sad meow.

Taking her old heat suppressants off the counter, she read the label and frowned.

Most effective in she-Cats under the age of twenty-five.

Of course it was. And here she was, thirty-three years old, unmated, and going through this alone. Again.

"Just in case," she murmured, and swallowed two pills before jumping in the shower.

Miracle of miracles, one hour and fifty minutes later, Annabeth was dressed, packed, and standing outside her condo. She waited for her driver to pick her up, and almost fell off her seat when she saw the gorgeous, stretched limo pull to a stop exactly three minutes later.

"Wowza," she purred, staring at the elegant vehicle.

The car was a beauty. Highly polished black paint

glittering in the afternoon sun, but it was the famous hood ornament that caught her eye. The shiny silver lady dubbed the stuff of legends.

If memory served, the woman who was the model for the infamous *Spirit of Ecstasy* pendant was involved in a tempestuous affair with the company's owner. Annabeth recalled the little she knew about it sadly. She loved collecting information, studying things that took her interest on the fly.

She had no idea Uzzi's connection would be picking her up in a luxurious Rolls Royce. Annabeth sighed, drawn to the dazzling beauty that was the brand's calling card. It was truly magnificent. Without even realizing it, Annabeth had stepped into the car's path and walked right up to the small object, reaching out a hand to touch it reverently.

"Stop!" a deep, rumbly voice commanded, and although she never listened to orders, Annabeth halted.

Her eyes were caught in the gleam of the Rolls Royce limousine's headlights, and she growled softly. Not in warning, she was shocked to discover. That growly little sound was more of a welcome to the owner of that deep, sexy voice. Her inner Lioness pushed against her skin, going completely belly-up as if waiting for rubs from the speaker.

"The hood will be hot," the male stranger warned.

The vibrations from his deep, husky words seemed to stroke along the exposed skin of her arms and legs. Annabeth was wearing a sleeveless blouse in a deep red color and a pair of short dress shorts for the drive. She felt soft, feminine, and pretty. For some reason, that had been important to her after she'd hung up with the driver.

She stood like a deer, *er*, make that Lioness, in headlights until the owner of that sultry voice stepped around the car. Holy hotness. Annabeth's lips parted slightly.

Now that was what a man was supposed to look like, she mused. Tall with wide shoulders, he wore a dress shirt and jacket, neatly pressed slacks, and black leather shoes. He looked professional, clean cut, and so damn sexy she almost sighed out loud.

Short, light brown hair with silver threaded throughout just at his temples topped his head and gave him a sophisticated air. He had sharp cheekbones, a straight nose, and powerful chin. His lips were a straight line, hard and uncompromising. Annabeth wondered if he ever smiled. What would she have to do to breakthrough that armor he wore? And no, she was not talking about his driver's uniform.

His blue gaze seemed to take her in from head to toe, and Annabeth registered his shock. But before she could decide if that was good or bad, he schooled his expression to remain indifferent.

Bummer.

Her inner kitty would have preferred knowing up front if she was in the running—wait. What? In the running for what?

No. NO. NO!

Annabeth did not go in for guys who looked sharper than a tack. And this guy looked that and more. Like some sexy college professor from one of those smutty romance books Toni liked to read when she thought no one was looking. Sophisticated or not, Annabeth could tell despite all his finery, the man was lethal, deadly, and fine as fuck.

"Miss Golden?" he said her name like a question, and she realized he was waiting for her to respond.

"Yes," she replied as he came around to stand just in front of her.

"I'm Hank Garret," he seemed to purr, and for a moment she thought he might be a Lion.

Then she took a deep breath and realized she was wrong. He was not a Lion. She smelled no fur on him, but Hank Garret was not human. Oh no. He was something else alright.

I'm yours.

The words he'd growled over the phone earlier replayed in her head, and she found herself nodding.

He was hers.

Mine.

Mate, her Lioness hissed.

OMG.

Realization dawned so brightly, she gasped. She could hardly wrap her head around it. He was here, and he was hers. Annabeth Golden had a mate!

Uncle Uzzi did it!

Smiling widely, Annabeth moved closer to him, invading his personal space. Wanting to touch, to taste, to vault into his arms, she was damn near breathless with joy. But then he sidestepped her, opting for her luggage instead of the embrace she was hoping for.

"Are these yours?"

"Yes," she replied confused.

Maybe he's shy. Maybe he needs words first.

Okay, we can do that, her Lioness suggested.

"So, you know Uncle Uzzi?"

Annabeth waited while he loaded the trunk of the beautiful vehicle. Her soon-to-be-mate was just bashful. That was okay. She could be that way too, sometimes. And to be honest, this was all kinds of overwhelming.

"He is my uncle," Hank clarified.

"Oh, wow. That is so cool."

Annabeth smiled again. Her heart was pounding furiously inside her chest. She couldn't believe it was going to be this easy.

Mate. Mate.

Mate. Mate. Mate.

Mate.

She sang in her head, but something was off. Why wasn't he gathering her up in his arms and laying claim to her lips like she so desperately wanted him to? Arousal spiked through her blood. He smelled so good, like male and musk and something wild. She wanted to get closer to him, to rub herself all over him and catch some of that scent on her skin.

Annabeth waited for him to close the trunk. When he did, she was more than ready. Time seemed to slow down as his cobalt eyes pinned hers with an intensity so hot, she thought she might burn to a crisp. Warmth filled her, and moisture pooled between her thighs.

"I can't believe Uzzi set this up after only one meeting. Your uncle must be a wizard," Annabeth purred, boldly invading his personal space for the second time, with no intentions of relenting.

He smelled intoxicatingly good. This close, Annabeth picked up on more nuances of his natural scent. It was like spring breezes, budding trees, and freshly laundered clothes. Arousing, addictive, and so damned tempting.

She wanted more. Her Lioness chuffed, begging her for a closer sniff. She wanted to rub her fur on him, to mark him with her own musk.

Kiss. Nibble. Bite—eeek!

Slow down, kitty.

Every instinct pushed her towards him. There was no patience or fear. No foolish trepidation or self-doubt. This was right. He was right. She felt it in the way her stomach flipped. Knew it in the tightness of her chest squeezing her runaway heart. Annabeth bit back her moan as her nipples tightened beneath the silk and lace confection she'd daringly donned for this drive.

Her own sex warmed and grew slick just being near the gorgeous stranger.

No, not stranger—mine.

He was so neat and refined. Annabeth's fingers itched just looking at him. Hell yes, she was definitely going to do something about his perfectly combed hair and unrumpled appearance. He was so clean, so neat. She could not wait to dirty him up.

Yes, please.

Annabeth was so going to love this. She licked her lips, waiting for his invitation.

Screw it, she thought.

Why wait?

He was hers. Had said so himself.

"Hank?"

"Yes?"

"Catch," she purred, and then she did the one thing she'd been dying to do since she saw the man.

She jumped on him.

Mine.

Rawr.

Chapter Four

Falcons have amazing sight. Gyrfalcons even better than most other subspecies.

It was simply fact. Some people said falcons' reactions were so perfect, so on point, it was almost as if the beasts were precognizant.

Not one to brag, but Hank sometimes wondered if he had that gift as well. Especially when he wore his feathers.

Larger than his wild Gyrfalcon cousins when he wore his feathers, Hank was a veritable speed demon. Hunting in his raptor's skin gave him a high he'd never felt anywhere else.

Pun intended.

It was part of the reason he loved fast cars. He'd tried planes in his youth, but they were simply too constricting. Hank needed to feel the wind when he moved. As a Falcon whose wingspan was over nine feet of pure feathered muscle, he preferred to be the one in charge of his dips and dives when it came to air travel.

Driving gave him the same elusive rush he felt when he was in his Shifter skin. The debate was still on. Fast reflexes or precognition.

If only there was a definitive way to find out. But psychic abilities aside, Hank rarely knew what to expect when going out on a job.

True, he was very discerning when he chose his own assignments, but in this case, there had been no choice.

Clearly, Hank had pissed off Uncle Uzzi. Therefore, he'd invoked that special privilege only he could get away with. In other words, he owed the man so much he would never deny him anything.

So, when he'd given Hank that envelope with instructions to take care of his client, of course, he'd accepted it politely. And when Uzzi left him with the Lioness' picture and phone number, he'd been ready if unwilling to perform his duty.

Anything to make amends to the man who had done so much for him. Uncle Uzzi was his rock when times were hard. The Witch's unwavering belief in him helped the young Falcon Shifter get through his rebellious streak with aplomb and dignity. He'd pushed him to do better. To be better. And he'd succeeded.

But even at his best, he could never have foreseen what the Fates, or his wily uncle, had in store for him on this day.

Ffuuck.

Hank's breath expelled from his lungs with a soft hiss. The woman was beautiful. There was no other word to suit the curvy goddess who stood in the glaring beams of his headlights, like she'd emerged from some ethereal mists for him and him alone.

Long legs, round hips, indented waist, full breasts, and soft, smooth-looking ivory skin. It shone as if she'd been bathed in moonlight, but maybe that was just a trick of the light?

The evening was still overcast and gray, and the headlights on his Phantom came on automatically. Swirling silver mists circled around her, and he blinked rapidly, trying to clear his vision.

He refocused, but nope, she was still there. Still gorgeous, and totally, inappropriately tempting. Her rich honey-colored hair was curled over one shoulder, and those eyes.

Fuck, they were beautiful.

They sparkled like golden discs in the low beams of the Rolls Royce, attracting his raptor and human sides with equal interest. Falcons did like shiny things, and Annabeth Golden was shiny. She was that and so much more.

Mine.

No.

Bad bird.

He wrestled with his inner beast, but the thing refused to listen. Fuck. This was impossible. She was not his. The female was a Lioness. Not a Gyrfalcon.

She. Was. Not. His.

This had to be some kind of trick. A test to prove his resolve to keep his promise to his father. Some sort of scrutiny or experiment set into motion by forces greater than himself for what? Hank did not know.

For a guy who held no particular beliefs aside from honor, integrity, and value, that was saying something.

Just a test. A cruel test. But a test nonetheless.

Picturing his purpose and intent in his mind, he pushed back his beast's primal initiative, which was to seize the lovely creature and make her his. It was difficult, but he had to fight his urges.

No, he issued the command, tethering his raptor to his will.

Hank had made a vow. A sacred promise to his parents to carry on their line after they'd fallen ill, succumbing to a rare disease that only affected Shifters who were also birds of prey.

He was going to mate a Gyrfalcon and have hatchlings. That was his pledge. And yet, for one single moment, in the silence that came with the twilight, Hank stood there, frozen in the headlights staring at the gorgeous female, and his resolve wavered.

Fuck.

It did more than that. It experienced earthquake-sized tremors. His chest was heaving, and still, he could not get any air into his lungs. The way those amber eyes had glowed as she blinked up at him stirred something deep inside of his soul. He'd never expected to feel this way.

It was more than lust, more than need. It was an enthusiastic, marrow deep yearning for the beautiful creature. Hank tried to still his erratic heartbeat. Tried to hide the long, hard evidence of his arousal which stood up, much as his Falcon perched in his mind at the first sight of the gorgeous female.

The Lioness stirred every single one of his deepest, most secret, hidden longings. Threatened to bring them to the surface with a mere smile or bat of her ridiculously long eyelashes.

She could be his undoing, he realized suddenly. But for some reason, that did not scare him. Quite the opposite. He was intrigued. Curious even. But that was an emotion best left to cats.

Hank was a Falcon. Hunter. Predator. Lethal. Extremely fast. And deadly. Very, very deadly. But birds and cats did not get along, did they?

Mate, his mammoth-sized bird screeched inside of his mind's eye.

Hank cleared his throat, uncertain of how to proceed. He knew she was not a bird of prey. Understood she was a she-Cat. Furry and gold, with sharp claws and teeth, though not as sharp as his talons and beak, he'd wager.

Let's find out, his animal pressed.

We could fly and run together. Through a field or in the city. I could watch her from the skies. See her cut through the meadows like a streak of gold in all her glory.

No! Shut up. She is not ours. We want feathers, not fur.

Hank insisted, trying to keep his inner animal restrained to more sane, safer thoughts than these. But who was he kidding? The woman was perfect.

Mine.

No.

Yes.

No, birdbrain. Think feathers, not fur.

Don't want another flighty female. Want her.

She is not ours.

She is.

No, he admonished quickly. But Hank sounded unsure even to himself.

Kak-kak-kak! His Gyrfalcon screeched angrily.

We don't have to worry about this now. We can discuss it later. Much later, he crooned to the bird, trying to soothe the furious fowl.

Of course, the hardness in his pants was pretty damn adamant the woman was something to him. It was bound to throw the whole mate possibility into question. Then it happened.

Literally.

The vexed female launched herself at him. And true to form, with no more than a grunt of surprise —he was a man, not a mouse after all—Hank caught the tasty little tidbit.

Thank the gods for his super-fast reflexes.

He'd barely had time to react verbally when she flung herself at him. Afterwards, his brain could only register that the enthusiastic bundle was warm and soft. Very soft. His grip was firmly secure to the glorious globes of her ass through the silky shorts she wore, and his dick grew even harder.

Holy fuck.

She felt good in his arms. Warm, soft, womanly, and so damn perfect. Her core practically singed his abdomen. Yes, she felt good there.

Purrfect, he thought and squeezed her ass involuntarily.

Soooooo good.

He dipped his head and took a deep breath against her neck. Her pulse was racing, and it was all he could do not to nip her flesh with his teeth. He should release her. Like now. But his stubborn inner bird was not ready to let her go.

Not yet. Maybe not ever. The lovely Lioness purred up against his chest. The feline female was also doing some sniffing of her own. That sexy rumble had his length longing to be freed and buried to the hilt between the thighs currently encircling his waist.

Sweet heaven, she was all curves and long limbs. He knew this because her fantastic body was currently wrapped around him. She clung to his solid form with all the tenacity of a giant boa constrictor. The kind he liked to eat when in his feathers.

Want to eat her, his raptor hissed unhelpfully.

Shhh!

Hank growled at his inner fowl. He needed to get a grip.

We have one. And it feels fantastic, the horny bird retorted, and again, Hank found himself suddenly squeezing her rounded bottom, grinding her against his cock.

"Stop," he growled.

He could hardly think with her warmth and scent surrounding him. The Lioness gave a deep sigh, nuzzling his neck with soft lips and warm breath in her exuberance. Any lesser man would've keeled over, not from her weight, slight as she was, but from her sheer strength.

But not him. Hank could more than handle her. The thought filled him with smug pride. He was no slouch. He was a predator, just as fierce and powerful as any Cat. He had everything this sexy little kitten needed.

Kak kak kak!

The closer she snuggled, the higher up her loose-fitting shorts rode. Her thighs were thick and smooth, and he realized with a groan his hands had worked their way beneath the silky fabric. Hank was now cupping her silky smooth, and uncovered skin, of her perfect ass.

Fuck.

If Hank could feel all that delicious flesh, that meant others could see it.

Grrr. Fuck no, his raptor screeched angrily.

He allowed her to slide down his body, ignoring the confused look on her face as he straightened her shorts. With firm hands on her deliciously dipped in waist, Hank put the female away from him.

"What are you doing? Should we go upstairs? I mean, I have to go to the convention, but we can do this, um, first—" she said breathlessly, her cheeks taking on a delightful pink tone as she spoke.

Fuck, she was cute. Adorable. And maybe more bashful than her exuberance said.

"I am sorry, but there seems to be some confusion."

"There's no confusion," she said disarmingly. "You said it already on the phone, lover. I'm yours. And you, you're my mate."

Her smile was bright, infectious, and totally sexy. What he wouldn't give to see those plump lips wrapped around his cock, cheeks hallowed in from taking his incredible girth and length from root to tip. Could she take all of him? Fuck, he hoped so.

Shit. Fuck.

He really had to stop all the pornographic images racing through his brain. Driving with a hard on was zero fucking fun. As it was, this trip was going to be downright uncomfortable.

"I am not your mate," Hank said firmly, trying to ignore the sudden pang that seized his heart when her lips dipped into a frown.

She should be smiling. Always. Someone should make sure she was happy and protected, safe and cherished. Some very lucky fucker should make certain every single inch of her was loved and properly worshipped.

But not him. Nope. That wasn't his job. He told himself that repeatedly, though unconvincingly.

Maybe if I say it to myself enough times, I'll believe it. Fucking hell.

That's what this trip was going to be. Absolute and utter hell. He shook his head.

"I think if you just wait a second, you will recognize what we are to each other," she tried again, ever hopeful.

Mine, growled his beast once more.

There went Hank's hope that all of this was just a

big misunderstanding. Both his Gyrfalcon and the lovely Lioness claimed they were mates.

Shit.

This mess had his uncle's signature all over it. Uncle Uzzi had bamboozled him. But this time he'd gone too far. His machinations got this sweet creature involved. She was still waiting on him to tell her it was a joke or something, but the words got caught in his throat.

Remember your vow.

His father's moue of distaste flashed in his brain. The man had worn that expression almost constantly in Hank's presence. Whenever he brought a friend home from school. When he'd told his dad about his love for cars. Whenever he'd talked about anything he liked.

Shit.

This would be another way of disappointing the old man, and he made a promise. What kind of man would he be if he did not keep his word?

Liar. Loser.

Every fiber of Hank's being was screaming at him to claim the luscious tidbit, but he would not give into his baser instincts. He couldn't.

"We are not mates."

"We are."

"Not," he insisted, realizing he sounded positively infantile.

The Lioness narrowed her eyes and crossed her arms, causing her fabulous breasts to push against the constrictive fabric of her blouse.

Should help her out of that, his randy raptor suggested.

Tight bras and shirts are rather uncomfortable, he agreed.

Perhaps both should be removed? Then he could caress and kiss the marvelous swells and see if anything else needed his attention.

No! Bad. Not ours.

Yesssssss.

"I am sorry, Miss Golden. There has been a mistake, you see, I'm engaged."

"You have a fiancée?"

"No," he said and ran a hand over his neck and tried to steady his breathing.

Of course, that only meant he got another whiff of her sweet strawberry scent, and fuck, it nearly brought him to his knees. She smelled like fur and candy and arousal and Hank was going to come in his pants if he kept breathing her in.

"I am engaged to be engaged," he told her in a rush. "That is, I have an appointment with the North

American Tower to find my mate. That's like a Pride, but for Birds of Prey—"

"Don't talk down to me," she snapped, and he had to admit her spunk kind of turned him on. "I happen to be the regional manager for *Eat Well Live Proud,* and I conduct business with the Tower regularly."

"My apologies," he said, biting back his grin.

"I'll have you know that EWLP provides top quality meat and fish for the Tower's annual shin dig. That's where you're going, I take it, and why you are driving me to the food con? Both are in South Jersey this year. Makes sense," she replied and expelled a harsh breath.

Hank nodded. That was one reason he'd agreed. Of course, he could call someone else to replace him as her driver. In fact, he probably should. Carter for instance.

Grrrrr.

His raptor was not having that. His Gyrfalcon was all kinds of pissed with him for denying them the feel of her in his arms. Damn, she was beautiful. But she was more than that too.

Annabeth Golden was full of surprises. Regional manager, huh? So, she was a hottie, quick with a smile, but also smart and feisty. All things he admired. But it didn't matter. They were not mates.

Keep telling yourself that, pal.

His raptor cried aloud inside the metaphysical plane where he rested and waited for Hank to call him. The powerful sound had him wincing, but he needed to stay focused.

"The point is this here," he said and gestured between them, "is a misunderstanding. I am all set to meet up with NAT's matchmaking department to find a suitable Gyrfalconess to ensure the propagation of our almost-endangered species. Surely, you can understand why we simply cannot happen."

"I see," Annabeth replied and narrowed her brilliant golden eyes at him.

For a moment, Hank wondered if she would cry. Fucking hell. He hated it when females cried. How could he soothe her and not touch her? And if he touched her, then it would all be over. Not that he would admit that out loud.

He waited a beat and watched a myriad of expressions flit across her face. Finally, determination won out, spreading across her features as she turned towards him. Damn, if he wasn't disappointed at being denied the chance to hold her once more.

"I understand," she said in a calm, professional voice.

"You do?"

"I said so, didn't I? Look, it's no problem. Let's get going. I would like to make it to the hotel early," she said.

"Are you sure you don't want another driver?" he offered.

Hank stood frozen, waiting for her to reply and his Gyrfalcon had a hissy fit at the thought. Too bad, he was not a monster. Hank had to give her the chance to get away from him after what was surely a terrible blow. Rejection hurt even if she was too proud to admit it.

Arrogant much? Maybe.

But he couldn't say his decision to mate a Gyrfalconess wasn't hurting him at this point either. His stomach lurched, chest tightened, and he couldn't swallow.

Fuck.

How could anyone be so damn pretty? And she was. She really was. Cute little nose. Gorgeous golden eyes. Pretty skin. Soft smile. Enticing lips. Decadent body.

This was so not helping. He closed his eyes and tried some yoga breathing, and *fuuckk,* all he managed to do was breathe her in.

Why did she have to smell so good? Like candy

covered sweetness, warm strawberry pie, homemade ice cream, and springtime.

He should call someone from the station to pick her up. Anyone else would be better. They could take her instead—*NO!*

No one drives her except me, growled the bird.

His raptor was possessive already. Definitely not a good sign, but Hank was still unsure. Truthfully, he had no idea what to do. Luckily, he did not have to do anything. The little Lioness took it out of his hands entirely, settling herself in the back seat of his limo.

"You ready?" she called impatiently.

"Uh," he replied.

Smooth. Real smooth.

"Look, we need to leave now. The sooner the better. I assume Uncle Uzzi explained this is a business trip," the sassy little bundle said and took out her laptop.

Ignoring his shocked stare, she slipped a pair of sexy-as-fuck tortoiseshell glasses on her straight button nose before flashing those golden beauties at him once more.

Did he say she looked sexy? Make that deadly. The woman could stop traffic with that getup. And judging from the satisfied gleam in her gaze, she knew it too.

"Yes, uh, he did," Hank said, responding to her original statement as he settled in the driver's seat.

"Good. Then I am also assuming he mentioned the little problem of me going into my heat cycle this week?"

The sound of her fingers flying across the keyboard was magnified tenfold as she dropped that little bomb in his lap.

Heat. Cycle.

He racked his brain for what he knew about it and came up with very basic info. Felines had a heat cycle. Unmated females who went into their heat needed protecting. Their sexy times pheromones amped up to like eleven, making every male within a ten-mile radius hard as stone and wanting to rut her like animals.

Fuck. Fuck. FUCK.

Hank had trouble making out her words, but his dick more than understood. She was going into heat, and he had everything she needed to take care of her. Fucking cock was already ready. Thing could punch a hole through a brick wall, it was so hard.

Most males reacted predictably to a female in heat. It was a biological imperative to want to service said female regardless of Shifter species, but she hadn't exactly gone into her heat yet.

Tell that to his primed cock, though.

Sigh.

Fucking hell. This trip was getting longer and more difficult by the second.

Heat cycle? You've got to be fucking kidding me. Uncle Uzzi is behind this.

Doesn't matter, his bird insisted.

Mine.

"I said, I will probably go into my heat in the next day or so, leaving me a short time to find *accommodations*," she told him.

"*Whaattt?* I mean, uh, I'm sorry, can you say that again?" he asked and tried for patience.

No.

He did not screech in an unmanly manner. That loud call was a perfectly normal sound for a bird of prey, *fuck you very much.*

"Just start driving, please," she instructed calmly.

He looked in the rearview, but her eyes were locked on her screen once more. Hank was not sure he liked her easy dismissal of him.

How could whatever the heck she was doing be more important than this discussion?

Uncle Uzzi must have known who she was. That

this female was his. And the man also knew of Hank's promise. He'd deliberately put him between a rock and a hard place.

A very hard place, he growled angrily, tapping his cock to calm the thing down.

Hank hit the steering wheel as he pulled into traffic with a screech of his tires. He was gnawing on the inside of his cheek, a habit he'd thought he kicked in high school.

"You don't have anger issues, do you? Cause I am just letting you know now, I come from a very large and rambunctious family. If this gets physical, I am pretty sure I can take you," Annabeth smirked, but she was still focused on her screen.

Take me? Yes, please. To bed. Or in the backseat. Anywhere you want, his raptor chimed in.

No. No. NO!

"I do not have anger issues," he replied between gritted teeth.

"Can you go any faster?"

"Why?"

"Well, I would like to get to the convention before my heat cycle begins. I don't know what you know about it, but it will get very painful for me. I need to find a suitable male, preferably a Shifter, to service me in my time of need. I would have asked you, but since you are, you know, *engaged to be engaged*, and we already had that unfortunate confusion about being mates, well, it's probably best left to someone else. Um, that was a red light," she said, and was she grinning? Fuck. Yes. She was.

MINE!

Kak kak kak!

His Gyrfalcon practically roared, the little beast was flapping his wings so hard, he was creating a fucking hurricane inside of him. Hank swerved into the other lane, ignoring the glaring horn of the fella in the red Jeep.

Fuck. Shit. Fuck. Shit.

It should be noted that Hank had a perfectly clear driving record. He'd never had an accident. Nor had he ever put a scratch or dent of any kind on any vehicle he drove. It was that whole Falcon eyesight or precognition thing again.

Yeah right, his inner fowl chuckled. *First time for everything.*

"What do you mean you need to find a suitable male? How?" he growled the question, hating himself for asking.

"Several of the businesses attending the con are Shifter run. All secret, of course, from the humans. I have some of their contact information and I'm currently going through the list of invited guests to see who fits the bill."

"Fits the bill?"

"Yeah. Look, Hank, this might be a joke to you, but when my heat starts, it's going to hurt. I'm a Lioness, not a human. I need a male who can handle me, so a checklist is necessary."

"What's on this checklist?"

Hank hated himself for asking but he could not stop himself. He watched her shrug in the rearview mirror and knew from her words she was being honest with him. In fact, the bit about it hurting—which she revealed twice now—rang of truth, and it gutted him to think of her in any kind of pain.

"Just some attributes. They aren't important," she whispered.

"Must be if you are checking them off some kind of list," he muttered.

"Fine. If you want to know, I am looking for someone strong. So, preferably, a Shifter, the larger the animal the better. He must be uninvolved at the moment. I will not be someone's little home wrecker. He should be physically acceptable, of course," she mumbled.

"So, you're looking at a list of guests for this con, picking out all the available men you know are

Shifters, and you plan on asking them to service you through your heat? Just like that? If this is some kind of fucking manipulation Annabeth, I can tell you right now, it won't work. I will not be forced to break a vow I made on my father's deathbed—"

Hank said, anger coiling in his gut.

"Oh, screw you, you conceited moron," Annabeth growled. "This is not about you!"

"Oh, no? Then why are you making a list of eligible men to fuck in the back of my limo after I rejected the notion of being your mate?"

Ouch. That fucking hurt. He looked at the raw pain and hurt on Annabeth's face, hurt that he put there, and Hank felt like throwing up. Hell, he'd only known her for like ten minutes, and already his instincts were all over the fucking place.

Shit. Shit. SHIT.

"Why am I making this list after meeting the man I thought was my mate and having him openly reject me? Hmm? How about, because Mother Nature and the Fates are a bunch of sadistic bitches, Hank? Does that answer the question?" she growled.

"Annabeth—"

"No wait, there is more," she said, and he felt her anger boiling from the front seat, and fuck, he knew he deserved it.

"Look—"

"Don't interrupt now. Where was I? Oh yes, well, I saw you, thought it would be fine, but then you said you're not mine. Okay then, I accept that. But it does not matter if you want me or not," she said with so much raw pain Hank wanted to punch himself in the face.

"It does not matter," she continued, "because in about twenty more hours, I'm gonna need me some dick, Hank! Whether or not you're my mate is completely fucking irrelevant! Ohmyfuckinggawd! Watch out!" Annabeth shouted.

A few minutes later, Hank was standing outside glaring at the new fire-hydrant-red scratch gracing the front right fender of his Phantom. He glared angrily, trying to absorb everything that had happened in the past twenty minutes.

Fuck.

His keen eyes spied a pair of high heels leading up to shapely ankles, and a pair of long, curvy legs outfitted in some silky and dainty as fuck shorts. Annabeth stood, leaning against the door, an amused smirk on her pretty face. She tapped the door with her long red nails.

"So much for a perfect driving record, like your website says."

"You googled me?"

"Of course, I did. Well, you comin', slick?" she asked.

Not yet, his bird replied.

Hank rubbed a hand over his face. The stubble on his cheeks was a surprise, but he supposed his emotions weren't the only things out of control upon meeting the little Lioness. Seemed his Shifter hormones were running amok as well.

"Best hop to it, lover. We are in for a long drive," Annabeth whispered, sliding back inside the limo, her pretty little feet disappearing last.

Was that a whimper that came from his throat as she disappeared behind the car door?

Fucking hell.

Chapter Five

It's him. He's mine. He doesn't want me.

Annabeth's heart was pounding double time as she pretended a nonchalance she sure as fuck did not feel. The male was her mate. Her actual, real life, deemed by the Fates themselves mate. But he didn't want her.

Her cheeks heated and as she stared into the reflection of the laptop she was pretending to work on, she saw herself flush a deep crimson as the painful truth hit her hard.

The word REJECTED went off inside her brain like a flashing road sign. The kind she always wanted to ignore on the side of the road that said things like *Sundays are for driving* or *Road Hogs Make Great Bacon.*

Yes, she always read the corny sayings, but still. Talk about distracting. This was why she refused to drive long distances. Annabeth was just no good at paying attention to things like her GPS.

Sure, taking out her laptop was a great cover, but regardless of what she'd told Hank-the-mate-that-never-was, as she'd now dubbed him, Annabeth was not perusing a list of prospective fuck buddies. She knew damn well who attended these events, and Annabeth was not about to boff Judd the Jerk, Archie McCullen's son from McCullen Cutlery, or Freddy Gennaro, witless heir to the restaurant linens laundering empire known as *Gennaro's Laundromatic*. They were the only two people at the event she could recall offhand who were born in the same decade as her. But they were not her type at all.

Hard, hard pass.

But, since she had her laptop open and was using her cell phone as a hotspot, Annabeth enlisted her sisters in a private chat to help come up with a solution. The Golden Lionesses were always involved in one another's affairs. They were her best friends, her cheerleaders, and, at times, her fiercest critics, and competitors.

Baby brother Georgie stayed out of it—he didn't

really stand a chance against any of them, but they still loved the little butthead.

Truth—all the Goldens were loyal. Annabeth knew she could depend on them, and that counted for everything. It was important that she get their input right now. She needed their support and love, and maybe, if she were lucky, they would know what she should do.

Initiating the private group message, Annabeth waited for someone to answer first. She sat there nervously changing the theme and color of the conversation to broken hearts and purple backgrounds.

Melodramatic? Maybe. But it seemed fitting.

Sad rawr.

Her inner Lioness was slumped on her side, dejected and brokenhearted. Silly feline didn't even know the man, but that kind of reaction from a fated mate was bound to hurt the beast even more than the human.

Sigh.

A request flashed in the corner of the screen, and Annabeth growled. There was only one person who was never ever allowed in a private Golden sister private messaging chat group, and that was their mother.

Patricia Golden was by far the busiest busybody of *busybodydom*. The worst tattle tale in the entire Blue Valley Pride. She had caused more trouble by her predilection for telling secrets, and rumor mongering than any other feline in Pride history.

For realz.

The woman could not keep a secret. Even worse, she wasn't above bribery, blackmail, and drugging her enemies to get her way. Especially if said enemies were trying to pussyblock her little princesses. Annabeth blocked her mother, then wrote in the private sisters only chat.

ANNABETH

Mayday Golden Girls! I am in desperate need of your wisdom, and all around awesomeness, for a sudden revelation that has proved devastating.

TONI

'Sup?

ADRIANNA

We killin' or buryin'?

ARIELLA

I still have the shovel in my car!

ANNABETH

Shh! I need you all to listen!

She typed faster than the rest of them, so she was able to get the whole sad story out in record time. And what a fucked up terrible story it was.

Annabeth had run into the infamous Uncle Uzzi. The man had delivered her mate to her door—literally. But the fuckface did not want her. He was sticking to some story that he made a promise to his father and now he was determined to mate one of his own kind.

TONI

A speciesist? No way, AB. I mean, dude who needs that shit?

ANNABETH

No, he is not a speciesist. Just confused. Thinks it is his duty to propagate the species.

For some reason, she felt obligated to defend her would-be-mate. After all, Hank could have waited until after they boned to deny what they were to each other. That would have been infinitely worse.

Maybe. But it would have been worth it, her inner kitty replied.

ADRIANNA

I say you tackle him.

TONI

She's right, AB. Crap. Where is the crying cat emoji?

ADRIANNA

I say we dress him up like the turkey he is, then roast his ass over a pit if you can't get him to change his mind.

ARIELLA

Ladies, please! Annabeth needs our help, not nutty suggestions. Look honey, you need to talk to him.

She was the first Golden sister who claimed to have met her mate. But like Annabeth, her guy was just not rising to the occasion.

TONI

Fuck that. Get naked and sprinkle sunflowers on your coochie. That should get him down to munching in no time. Then when he's busy muff diving, pull a 69 and go rocket chomping. Just when he's about to blow, scratch, and bite his fine ass. Mark him. Then he'll be all yours.

ARIELLA

Yes, for the pussy snacking!

ADRIANNA

Personally, I like a good finger bang simultaneously with clitoral stimulation via glossa.

ARIELLA

What's via glossa?

TONI

It means she liked the licky lucky on her kitty's clitty.

ANNABETH

You guys are sick. And that is way TMI, Toni!

"What's going on? Did someone get back to you already?" Hank asked, and her eyes darted to the rearview mirror only to freeze when she met his cobalt stare.

Did he have to have such gorgeous eyes? Blue was her favorite color. And that particular shade of blue was like the prettiest bit of stained glass from her favorite window at the Blue Valley Non-Denominational Chapel on Prism Street.

Sigh.

"Nunya," she muttered.

"Really? You're going to *nunya business* me?" he scoffed.

"If the shoe fits," she added, refusing to give him anymore ammo to shoot her with.

ADRIANNA

What's he look like, anyway?

ARIELLA

I bet he's like this sexy biker.

TONI

That's your fetish, Ari. (insert wolf emoji- fuck I can't find any emojis).

ANNABETH

Okay. He is hot. But he's more like hot nerdy with Rhett Butler silver streaked hair.

ADRIANNA

What about his package?

Fighting her telltale blush, she snapped the screen closed guiltily.

Hubba hubba.

She didn't really know about his package—okay, that was not entirely true. There had been a whole hugging thing back at her condo where she totally felt his, *er,* bulging big boy and it sure was promising. Not that Annabeth was a size queen or anything. Still, she appreciated a man who was packing. And so did Miss Kitty, apparently.

Grrrr.

They'd been driving on the parkway for a little while now, and traffic was crawling. Fuck. This was boring. No small talk to make. I mean, what was she going to say—*so, is it my fat ass that turns you off or my face?*

Ugh. No thank you. She did not even want to know. And fuck that, anyway. Annabeth was pretty awesome, if she did say so herself. Mr. Uptight could fuck right the fuck off.

Hmm. But she was soooo bored. The cars were practically stopped. Like the parkway could basically be called a parking lot. Oooh. She hadn't even mentioned the whole hydrant thing. Maybe she could ask him.

"So, is it a big scratch?"

"Excuse me?" Hank frowned.

"From the hydrant."

"Oh. No. It will probably buff right out."

"Oh, cool. I assume that kind of thing happens all the time."

"Uh, no. First time, actually," he replied between gritted teeth.

"Oh," she said, and tried to hide her grin.

Maybe he wasn't as immune as he pretended, she mused. After all, the call of a fated mate was intense, and she was about ninety-nine percent certain he was hers.

Maybe her sisters were right, in a roundabout kind of way. Maybe she just had to break through that armor of his. Even if she had to kick through it with her size ten heels.

"Uh, do you know exactly when your heat cycle is going to begin? Like, will you get some kind of warning?" Hank asked, surprising her with the question.

"Are you asking if my hooha will start making some sort of beeping noise, like an alarm?"

"What? No! That's not what I meant," he said, and snorted a laugh.

The sound was cute, and he looked surprised he'd made it. She wondered how much he actually laughed out loud if the sound of his own laughter shocked him. Annabeth bit back her own grin.

For some reason, she was proud she'd made him laugh like that. Wondered if she could do it again. Hell, even her animal was greedy for her to try. She liked his laugh. Wanted to hear it some more.

"Um, seriously, by my calculations, I should be in full heat by Friday evening," she answered honestly.

"At the last rest stop, I did some research. There are pills you could take—"

"I know," she said. "And I've taken them. They get less and less effective as the female ages. Of course, there are some experimental elixirs. Actually, my sisters are trying to contact the Witch and scientist who make it. Their place is in this direction, and they should get back to me soon if they have any availability. I understand it is still in the development stage."

"I'm sorry, I was just trying to help."

"No, I get it. You want to make sure I am not trying my feminine wiles, or in this case, the fact of my biological makeup to trap you," she murmured, and tried not to get her feelings hurt when he didn't deny it.

This conversation was a tad embarrassing, but Annabeth wanted Hank to know she was not trying to trick him. She wanted him to find her more appealing, not less.

"What do you mean about age? You are not old," he said.

Smart man.

But the Fates would not dare give her someone

dull. Annabeth was smart as a whip. Incidentally, she was also not afraid to use one as one previous boyfriend had found out. Unfortunately, she discovered *safe words* only after her whole BDSM phase.

But what were a few restraining orders from guys who couldn't deliver, anyway? She didn't need them. She finally found her mate. Now, she just had to land him.

"I'm thirty-three. By Pride standards, I should have been mated by now with cubs."

"So, why are you single?" he asked.

"Really? We both know why, Hank. Even if you're determined to ignore it."

"Look, it's not that you aren't nice or pretty, Annabeth. I am sure you're a very special woman—" Hank started.

"What do you mean?"

"You're a lovely Lioness, Annabeth," he said quietly.

Truth.

"Just not lovely enough," she replied sadly.

"It's not you," he whispered.

"I am so sorry. It's just, I made a promise—"

"Say no more. I get it. You don't have to keep telling me you don't want me, you know. I am quite intelligent, and English is my first language."

"First? How many do you speak?" Hank asked.

"Seven," she said, noting the way his eyes widened. "Not all felines are flippant. And you know, you could be less obvious about being a speciesist."

"What? I am not! And I never said—"

"Yeah, you didn't have to. It is written all over your face."

"What is?"

"You, Hank Garret, are a prude. And you are prejudiced against feline Shifters."

"What? No! I made a vow to ensure the survival of my species. That does not make me prejudiced," he scoffed loudly, only proving her point.

"Actually, it kinda does. You think we're all a bunch of silly, lazy Lions who do nothing all day but lick ourselves and lay down in the sun!"

We do not, her Lioness butted in.

She only groomed herself outdoors on special occasions and during vacations. Annabeth wisely kept that tidbit to herself during this conversation.

Truth was every Shifter group had its own quirks and preconceptions of other groups. Just like normals.

Some things were based in truth or experience, others simply assumed. Like most misconceptions, it caused a lot of strife in her mother's heyday. But Annabeth had thought with the emergence of the next millennia, Shifters would have outgrown that kind of uncivilized behavior.

Sadly, they weren't that evolved yet. But she had hopes for the future of *Shifterkind*, and the other inhabitants of the multiverse as she knew it.

"I am not a speciesist, but I have a duty. Before they died, I promised my parents I would mate a Gyrfalconess. I owe it to them," he shook his head in denial, but she saw right through him.

"As for the whole Lion preconceptions, it's just, from what I have experienced—"

"Ha! But that is just it," she hissed. "You have *no* experience of *me*, Hank Garret. There I was, ready to let you claim me based on instinct alone, and I knew nothing about you."

"That was a mistake, Annabeth. I am sorry. I know Uncle Uzzi meddled, and I will speak to him. It was not right of him to get you involved in our little argument. But I still don't know—"

"What? You don't know me? No shit. I don't know you either, but I was willing to take a chance on you."

"Annabeth—"

"No," she snapped, really angry now. "I mean, you

act like a Lioness couldn't possibly meet your Gyrfalcon standards, whatever they are. But what if you can't meet mine? Did you even consider that?"

"What?"

"*Ohmygawd!* Look at your face. This never even crossed your mind," she said with a shake of her head. "So, Hank, how many languages *do you speak?* How many degrees *do you hold* and from what universities? Do you value family? Who are your friends? Are you always so uptight? Do your clothes always have to look so neat?"

"My clothes? What does that have to do with anything? Look, it is not personal, Annabeth—"

"Not personal? How could *rejecting me* not be personal? Whatever, lover, I'm sure you have your issues too," she replied and glared at him in the rearview mirror.

She caught sight of herself too and could have screamed her fury. Annabeth's hair looked wild and her cheeks red. Her eyes glowed gold with her Lioness, a further testament to her riled up state. Fuck. She was going to lose her shit.

"Seriously, whatever, Hank. I never wanted a tight ass for a mate either."

"I am not a tight ass, Annabeth," he growled.

Oooh, goody. She was starting to piss off the pretty birdie.

"Liar. I bet you'd go nuts if I leaned over the back of that chair and mussed your hair."

He sucked in a sharp breath behind his teeth, making a clicking sound, and Annabeth snorted.

"See? You total bonehead. There are a million things I could have assumed about you from our first meeting, but I didn't, Hank, and even after all this, I won't."

"Oh yeah, Saint Annabeth? Why is that?"

He was breathing heavily, and his cheeks were flushed with anger. She wondered what he'd look like if he really exerted himself. Like between the sheets. Or against the wall. Anywhere really.

Sigh.

Looks like we rile him up plenty, after all, her inner Lioness thought with a satisfied purr.

"I am reserving my opinion until I receive further information," she replied primly.

"I see," he said, eyes on the road.

A few minutes later, the Rolls rolled to a stop as traffic just basically shut down. Red and blue lights were blinking up ahead, and it looked to Annabeth as if traffic was being directed to take the exit.

"What's going on?" she asked.

He didn't answer right away, but he made the radio louder and frowned as he turned to an AM station.

"Okay, so traffic isn't moving, and they are shutting down the highway due to a chemical spill ahead."

"Oh no," she said. "Is there a way to go around it?"

"Not really. It's probably best if we just fuel up, get some food, and stop for the night."

"Okay, I'll find a hotel," she grumbled.

"Don't bother. I already know one. It's Shifter owned, I've stayed there before."

"Fine."

"Fine."

Annabeth turned her head and watched the scenery go slowly by as he expertly maneuvered the Rolls behind the slowly moving traffic off the highway. There was no way for him to exceed the speed limit, but she could tell he wanted to. Annabeth bit her lip nervously. Music played low in the background, and for some mysterious reason, Hank kept the partition down. She'd thought for sure he would've closed it as soon as she got inside the beautiful vehicle. But he didn't.

After her tantrum, she kinda wished he would.

No, you don't.

Yes, I do, she told her she-Cat.

Liar liar.

Annabeth bit back her groan. Was there anything as terrible as being rejected? She knew exactly why the big, sexy raptor didn't want her. For fuck's sake, and here she'd always prided herself on being such an upbeat girl, proud of her curves. But just this once in her life, she wished she was fine-boned and petite.

Annabeth was anything but. Big and thick, though she had a certain feline grace, Annabeth knew damn well Falcons, and the other Bird Shifters, were all light and thin.

Pretty and petite. Not like me. Not by a long shot.

Okay, well, she was pretty. She wasn't stupid or crazy. Annabeth knew she was cute. Had heard it often enough, but who wanted to be cute and single at thirty-three?

Ugh.

Why couldn't she have been fated to mate with a Bear? Bears were totally into thick chicks. Ah, but no. She had to be fated to mate a guy who literally would rather eat bird seed than the nice, fat, juicy steaks she loved.

Rare, of course.

With plenty of freshly ground black pepper and sea salt sprinkled on top.

A little melted butter with a sprig of rosemary and a clove of freshly crushed garlic.

Voila.

Purrfection.

Damn, she really liked steak. Speaking of which, her stomach took that opportunity to let its request be known. Annabeth sighed and wished the door would just open so she could roll out to her demise on the lonely highway.

Really? Now my stomach is growling like I'm some hungry teenaged boy. WTF.

"We're almost there. The hotel has a great little diner attached," Hank told her, his expression one of concern.

"Great," she murmured, refusing to meet his stare.

Humiliation was not a good look on her. Besides, she did not want to see the pity she was sure would be there in those otherwise perfect blue eyes of his.

Sad yowl.

Chapter Six

*F*uck. *Fuck. FUCK.*

Hank's brain had been seesawing between the overused curse word and the equally obnoxious, single-syllable word that had been stuck on repeat since he met the beautiful feline—*mate.*

Only, inside Hank's overly obsessed mind, it was more like *mate, mate, mate,* slight pause, then, *fuck, fuck, fuck.*

Both words operating on alternating channels of repeat in his now throbbing head. What was he supposed to do in this situation?

Really, he should be pissed at Uncle Uzzi. The elderly Witch knew better than this. He was a stubborn bastard at the best of times, but did he have to bring this female into all this mating nonsense?

Hank had promised his parents, and that was the end of the discussion, as far as he was concerned. Fated mates had never been part of their infrequent chats. Of course, when he thought back to the cold relationship that existed between his mother and father, he cringed.

He could not recall a single memory where his parents held hands or behaved with affection towards one another. They hadn't even slept in the same room. A fact he'd forgotten until just then.

A quick glance in the rearview, and he noted Annabeth looking out the window. Lost in thought, she was relaxed and oh so lovely. He took a moment to study her features.

Her oval face was so beautiful. Perfectly symmetrical, drawing his eye effortlessly. She had a stubborn little chin and a smooth, blemish free complexion.

Her eyebrows had the cutest little arch, and that bow of a mouth had him thinking dirty thoughts in no time. The things he would love to do to and with that mouth.

Dear gods.

Kak kak kak.

His Falcon agreed wholeheartedly. The raptor intent on staking his claim on the sexy little minx. When the little Lioness had mentioned her heat cycle, his cock had immediately stood at the ready.

One sultry, seductive mate in her heat? Why, yes, please. I will take her!

Why the hell wouldn't he relish the thought? Just think of the little golden furred and spotted feathery young they would have! A beautiful mix of healthy, happy, well-loved offspring. And fuck yes, he knew immediately, she would be warm and loving to her young.

Maybe if he was lucky, to him as well.

Sure, it was way too early to assume the emotion for himself. She did not love him. She did not know him. But he knew instinctively she would love their babies.

Just as he would. He would never want his children to grow up in an affectionless, cold home. A home where the parents could hardly stand each other, much less, the offspring they'd created.

Like our home, supplied his Gyrfalcon.

Fuck.

That wasn't true. Was it? And if so, why would he doom his children to the same fate?

Hank shook his head to clear it of all these

unwanted thoughts as he pulled into *Big Bob's Hotel* parking lot.

The Moose Shifter had a very peculiar sense of humor that led to his place resembling a sort of road sign cemetery. In other words, the guy stole road signs.

Sometimes, folks brought them to him, and he hung them up on the exterior of his joint. He sure loved a good joke, and Hank appreciated his sarcasm. As far as roadside hotels went, it was not luxurious. But it was clean, and the food was good.

"Big Bob's Hotel?"

Hank stilled, waiting to hear derision or anger in her voice, instead, he was gifted with a soft snort as she laughed into her hand.

"Ha ha! Does that sign say 'God' and is it pointing up?"

His lips quirked up in a smile as Annabeth continued to read, and laugh, and yes, she snorted again too. What could he say? The sounds were adorable, and he might have slowed down so she could look her fill.

"Yeah, Bob is a character. His wife Rosa runs the diner."

"Really? Good. I am starved," she unbuckled her

seat belt and climbed out of the car before he could open the door.

That kind of rankled his animal, but then she sighed and stretched, bending over in those short shorts to touch her toes. Her peach-shaped ass thrust out and his chest rumbled appreciatively. There was nothing compared to this woman's shapely legs and curvaceous body.

Hubba hubba.

He growled again, hiding it with a cough when she whipped her head around. Honey-colored strands danced in the night air, like golden tinsel and her eyes glowed with her beast for a second. He was sure he saw her smirk before she straightened. The little minx knew exactly what she was doing to him.

Grrr. So let her already, his raptor insisted, but Hank shushed the animal.

After he convinced her he had it, Hank carried her luggage firmly in his hand, He also withdrew a package wrapped in brown paper from the trunk and walked beside her to the small building labeled office. The huge Moose Shifter was sitting behind the desk apparently sleeping, but his shaggy head shot up, and a smile graced his rough looking features the second he spied Hank.

"If it isn't my favorite prince of the peacocks! Get

over here," growled Bob, pulling Hank into a hug, and lifting him clear off the ground.

"Ooof!" he muttered. "Put me down, you big Moose! Bob! Here, I got you something," Hank grumbled, but he was grinning as he handed the brown-wrapped package to the giant.

"Looks like you got me two somethings," he said, waggling his eyebrows at Annabeth, who blushed prettily, and giggled.

"Now, don't you go gettin' me in any trouble, Big Bob," Annabeth laughed, and it was like wind chimes sounding happily in the breeze.

"I hear your Rosa is the best cook in these parts, or she would be *if* she had the best products."

"How do you mean?" Bob's smirk faltered as he unwrapped his gift.

The Moose took a moment to admire the road sign that read *Mount Maverick: Only Folks with a sense of humor are welcome, because our Mountains Are Hill Areas.*

Bob grunted a sound that was close to a laugh, then turned to the sassy little Lioness just as Annabeth started her pitch about *Eat Well Live Proud.* Hank had to hand it to her. She had grace and finesse, and she knew when to push and when to back off.

The fact she was smiling up at Bob and charming the pants off the Moose shouldn't have bothered Hank. Especially not when Bob's features softened, and he stared starry-eyed at the little minx.

The man was old enough to be her father and mated to boot. But Hank's raptor still chirped incessantly. The Moose was too close to the female, too interested. Jealousy was not a good look on Hank.

He closed his eyes to count to ten—*remember the yoga breathing.*

Fuck. Off. His Falcon snarled.

Hank tried again to quell that possessiveness he'd started feeling over the pretty woman. He had no rights or claims on the female. But fuck, he was not expecting to be this easily riled by her.

"I see," Bob replied when Annabeth was finished explaining all about her company's offerings.

"Tell you what, I'll get you guys a key for your room. Then you and Hank here can head over to Rosa's for some grub. If she says yes, you got our business," he winked.

"That's great, Bob, but we need two rooms," Hank supplied.

"Oh," Bob said scratching his head.

"Sorry, I assumed. Gee, this is embarrassing," he grumbled, "You see, the thing is, there's a soccer tournament in town, and I am fully booked. Only have the one room left."

Hank stilled. His Gyrfalcon whistled appreciatively, the sound morphing into a growl at the prospect of being alone with the curvy Lioness.

This could not be happening. He was already hard pressed not to pin her against the wall and have his way with her, but that would probably lead to all sorts of complications. As attractive as he found the female, she was not for him.

Confusion, lust, and a constant threat to undermine his overall peace of mind had Hank standing there like a moron, instead of answering his long-time friend. Bob scratched his head and cleared his throat again, but Hank just could not move for the life of him.

It was Annabeth who smiled brilliantly at the Moose and took the key, nodding her thanks. She also grabbed her roll-along suitcase from his feeble grip and walked, angrily, if her ramrod straight back was any indication, outside to the room they would have to share. Number one eleven right on the ground floor.

Fuck.

"Uh, thanks, Bob," he muttered and hurried after her.

The seductive sway of her hips was hypnotic as she hurried along the concrete walkway. He knew from the set of her shoulders she was pissed, but the sour note of embarrassment that marred her otherwise delightful scent brought a hint of shame to him.

He'd done that to her. Put her in this impossible position, and he had no idea how to apologize for it.

"Annabeth," he said her name once she arrived at the door to the hotel room.

"I'm sorry—"

"That's great," she said flippantly, with her back to him. "You're sorry. As usual. And I am hungry. Also as usual," she added with a self-deprecating chortle.

"What does that mean?" he asked, baffled. "Was that some kind of remark about your weight? Annabeth, there is nothing wrong with you—"

"Hank, please, I just can't take this right now. I'm going to go grab something to eat. You can join me for dinner or not. That's entirely up to you. I don't want to hear what you think about my weight or my person, or anything about me right now. Be sorry or don't. I don't care. I'm going to stow my bags and walk to the diner."

Her eyes were glowing, and fuck, she looked beautiful. But he'd hurt her again, and he'd never felt so low. This was an impossible situation, and Hank did not know what to do.

"I can sleep in the car," he offered, though truthfully, he did not look forward to the prospect.

"Like I said, your call," she replied, and left her suitcase against the wall, strolling past him without looking back.

Shit.

That could've gone better, he mused as he dropped his bag and walked after her. He had to hand it to her once again. Outwardly, the feline looked completely unruffled.

She smiled cheerfully at the few people milling about outside. There were a few kids in soccer gear accompanied by their parents. They were loitering around the parking lot and courtyard, kicking a ball while the parents hung out.

Fathers mostly. Without their wives. Males who seemed to think they could ogle his curvy little Lioness while their kids were busy dribbling their balls up and down on the sidewalk.

Hold up, he frowned.

She is not my little anything.

Is too.

Mine, his raptor insisted.

"Heads!" a small voice yelled, but before he could

even move, Annabeth jogged forward.

Even on heels she was nimble, fielding the ball and sending it back to the little boy with a smile and wave. But what did he expect? She was graceful as a cat should be.

Lovely.

"Nice moves," one bold father said, but he gulped and turned around when Hank lifted his lip and growled.

"Thanks," Annabeth waved and kept walking, ignoring Hank completely.

"Isn't it late? Shouldn't those kids be in bed?" he grunted as he stepped forward to open the door for Annabeth.

"Thank you," she murmured and shrugged past him.

Her sweet strawberry flavored fragrance invaded his nostrils once more. His beast growled and the human side of him wanted to bask in the warm, inviting scent. Why did it have to be strawberries? The small red fruit was his favorite, of course. Even more so when used in pies and goodies.

Her particular scent reminded him of hot-from-the-oven turnovers drizzled in icing and sweet enough to send him into ecstasy once the flavor hit his tastebuds.

Finger. Licking. Good.

Bet she's sweeter, his bird insisted.

Let's find out.

"Hi, table for two?" a young waiter asked.

He blushed furiously as he tried, and failed, not to stare at Annabeth's magnificent bosoms outlined in her high-necked top.

"Yes, please," she replied and smiled kindly, but Hank growled at the young man, *sniff,* make that Buck.

There were plenty of Deer Shifters in that particular neck of the woods so near the pine barrens. Bob's was known in the supernatural world as a Shifter friendly establishment. He hired plenty of supes and rented rooms without too many questions.

It was also rumored the Moose knew the names of some handy cleaners nearby. Not the usual dry cleaners a businessperson on the road might need. But something more suited to supernaturals who were doing their best to live and hide among the world's normals.

It was why this inn was one of Hank's favorite places to crash. In fact, Bob had already called someone to fix the scratch on Hank's limo without raising even one of his bushy eyebrows.

"Hank!" the screech that sounded from Rosa had Hank smiling at the short, round woman who was warm and friendly to all and sundry.

"Hello Rosa," he said and offered her a smile and returned the friendly hug.

His smile widened when the woman embraced Annabeth as well. The Lioness grinned and laughed at the friendly gesture.

"What's your name, *bonita*?" Rosa asked.

"Hi, I'm Annabeth Golden."

"Well, my Bob was not lying when he said you were just the prettiest little thing. Come on, let me feed you, then you can tell me about your proposal," she said and winked.

A few minutes, and many platters later, Hank and Annabeth sat quietly as they digested. It was a companionable silence. The kind he'd often imagined sharing with someone he was in a relationship with. Odd that he'd pictured her as the type to feel it necessary to fill the air with silly nonsense.

But she'd proved him wrong. It seemed the little Lioness was full of surprises and secrets. Like the fact she loved salsa, but it had to go on the bottom of her fajitas with the sour cream and guacamole on top.

Cute. Very cute.

But so was everything else she did. Like the careful way she added lime juice to her hot sauce or the way she'd used a napkin to wipe her fingertips and lips after every bite.

He wondered what other little interesting facts he'd discover about her on this short trip. Hank frowned. It was too short now that he thought about it.

Doesn't have to be, his bird butted in.

"Oh my," Annabeth sighed and patted her stomach in satisfaction. "Rosa, those were the best fajitas I have ever tasted. Your salsa verde is da bomb!"

"I told you," Rosa said proudly and sat down to join them for dessert and coffee, along with Bob.

Hank had enjoyed the dinner almost as much as simply eating it with Annabeth. He was happy to see she was not going to try to hide her healthy appetite. He hated the habit most female Bird Shifters had of ordering small salads when dining out.

Hank was a predator, and he had a healthy appetite. Gyrfalcons were hunters, like Lionesses, he mused. He appreciated meat in all forms, as well as fruits and berries. Annabeth's reaction when he'd asked for the same order as her had amused him greatly.

"*I ordered a double portion steak fajita combo with all the trimmings and sides,*" she'd said, as if he didn't hear her correctly when she spoke to the young Buck.

"*I know,*" he'd replied.

"*You eat meat?*" she'd asked.

"*I'm a Gyrfalcon, love, of course I eat meat,*" he'd returned.

The endearment that had slipped out of his mouth went thankfully, unnoticed by the gorgeous female. And they spent the rest of the meal in almost silence, though she had remarked on the proposed length of their trip.

"*So, no more than like an hour tomorrow, right?*"

"*Yes, if the parkway is clear. I can try to speed if you like—*"

"*No, that's okay. I mean, I am fine with the pace.*"

Hank sensed some tension on her side. Wondered if it was because they were stuck at a rather unfortunate impasse.

Uncle Uzzi had really done it this time. He made a mental note to send his well-meaning uncle an email once they got back to the hotel room. He hated the idea that Annabeth, though she showed no signs of being upset, should suffer because of Uzzi's stubborn insistence he knew best who Hank should mate.

"Just imagine what your recipes would taste like if you were using superior ingredients. Like the organically raised, grass fed, non-GMO beef, as well as other proteins, we offer at *Eat Well Live Proud*," Annabeth began.

Hank turned his head to listen as she began to expel endorsements from other chefs about EWLP products for Rosa's benefit. Bob already looked besotted with Annabeth's wit, and to be honest, she was too adorable for words. Rosa narrowed her eyes and leaned back against her man.

"We get wholesale prices?"

"You get fair prices for far better ingredients than what you have now. As an added bonus, it should be noted that once these restaurants and hotel chains," she started and turned the tablet she seemed to carry everywhere around to show Rosa and Bob some of her client list, "started using our products, they saw a fifteen percent increase in orders, and a surge in higher ratings and reviews everywhere online. Great food and more ratings mean more customers. For hotel owners, it means more people reserving rooms and even more return customers."

"I'm impressed," Rosa said, then turned to confer with Bob.

"You are good at this," Hank whispered, noting

the faint blush that crept along her neck and spread to her cheeks at his praise.

He wondered just how far the blush would travel. It would coat her plump breasts, and soft belly, down to her thighs, and the treasure between them. Wouldn't he love to find out?

Yes. Let's.

For fuck's sake. Why couldn't his raptor shut the hell up and forget the female?

Cause she is our mate.

No. Impossible. She was not a Gyrfalconess, therefore, not his mate.

Doesn't matter.

He'd made a promise. A sacred vow.

You owe it to yourself to follow your heart.

She was a Lioness. A fluffy, foolish feline who loved pranks and chaos. Not something Hank relished.

She is lively, voracious, and fun. We would do well with her. She will bring us joy.

On and on the arguments went. Back and forth inside his head with his raptor until he was getting looks from the other three adults at the table.

"I think we have a deal," Rosa was saying, lips pursed as she noted the untouched slice of flan on his plate.

Not wanting to cause an incident, he picked up his spoon and took a healthy bite. That at least earned him a smile from one of the females at the table. Annabeth, however, kept her eyes firmly away from his. To his unexpected dismay.

Once he'd paid for the meal, insisting despite her arguments they should split it, they returned to the room.

"Look," she turned to him, "I don't want to make this awkward. So, I have a solution for our sleeping arrangements."

"What's that?"

Hank stood and swallowed while she walked to the bathroom. She didn't bring any clothes with her, and the idea she intended to sleep in the nude had his cock standing up in an awkwardly inappropriate salute.

"When I tell you, I want you to count to thirty, then open the door."

"Uh—" He had no idea what to say.

Nerves assailed him. Did she want sex? Could he do that and remain whole? Doubts and fears, and most of all, unmitigated lust, surged through his body. The female was close to her heat cycle.

She'd said as much. Perhaps he could do her a service and take the edge off himself as well. No strings, he thought, frowning hard at the insinuation. Still, Hank nodded. Even felt a modicum of relief when she visibly relaxed.

He'd never hurt or injure a female knowingly. Not physically, mentally, or emotionally. No real man would, in his honest opinion. But how was he to remain sane if he slept with this vivacious woman?

Fated mates. We're fated mates.

Her voice rang through his head, and he tried sitting on the bed while he listened to the water running in the bathroom. Hank could not sit still. Pacing back and forth, he wiped sweaty hands on his pants.

Shit.

He'd never felt like this. Like a teenager about to see his first boob. His dick throbbed, heart wrenched, and stomach twisted. He was going crazy. That was the only logical explanation.

The sudden knock on the bathroom door had his head turning to the wood portal.

"Hank?"

"Yes."

"Okay, count to thirty," she said softly.

Hank closed his eyes, counting to ten. He could almost see her. All soft skin and ample curves.

Would her large breasts be tip-tilted? Would her nipple be pink or dusky? Would she taste like the strawberries her scent seemed to always carry?

He could hardly wait to discover the answers for himself. Walking forward on shaky legs, Hank's right hand reached out to turn the cool brass knob. This was it. His cock pulsed, pushing against the fabric of his pants. His brain kept playing erotic little snippets of all the dirty things he wanted to do to and with the supple feline.

Get a grip, he told himself, and turned the handle.

Shock had his eyes opening wide as he took in the sheer beauty that greeted him. Fuck. He was a total moron.

"Annabeth," he whispered, falling to his knees to take in the golden Lioness in all her furry glory.

The enormous she-Cat moved forward, butting her head against his shoulder. She was so sleek and stunning. Muscular and powerful with enormous claw-tipped paws that retracted as she moved, and huge fangs she flashed at him briefly when she growled. They were currently concealed, but he was very aware of their presence.

Powerful. Stunning. Hunter. Predator. Warrior woman.

Hank had never seen anything as beautiful as

Annabeth in her Lioness form, unless you counted Annabeth on her human legs.

"Can I?" he asked permission, raising a hand to touch her.

He waited until she pushed her head into his palm. A smile broke out across his face as he petted and tested the soft, thick fur on the ruff around her neck. It got thinner but no less lovely on her back and chest. Her beast purred, playfully knocking him to the ground before leaping over his body and settling on the bed.

Now he knew why Bob reinforced them. Her Lioness was at least seven or eight hundred pounds of pure muscle. She chuffed quietly. Her amber gold eyes glowed in the dim light of the room, and Hank knew what she waited for.

"Alright, smart lady," he said, and began stripping away his clothes.

Nudity was natural for Shifters, and he did not shy away from her golden star. Within seconds, the familiar hum of magic washed over his skin and before he took his next breath, he was in his feathers.

Gyrfalcons in the wild were about half the size of Hank's Shifter form. His raptor was stocky and large, muscular, with lethal talons on his feet. He had an almost ten-foot wingspan, and his feathers were various hues of brown, white, and gray, with spots on his chest.

He whistled low and clear, directing her attention to him. He needed to fly, wanted to fly, and preen for her enjoyment. But he knew it was too risky there.

Maybe someday we can run and fly together.

But his thoughts turned sad when he recalled his determination to mate with another of his kind. Sorrow swept through him, but the sound of her chuffing brought his head up.

At least they would have this, he thought. Amazed by her foresight, he hopped onto the bed, settling next to the beautiful Lioness. They could have this night together, sleeping side by side in their animal forms. He wouldn't be breaking his vow that way, and that thing inside of him that had been raging against his reserve ever since he laid eyes on her finally quieted.

For now, at least.

For now.

Chapter Seven

TONI

How goes it on Operation Claim the Cock?

The message from Toni popped up on Annabeth's laptop screen while she was checking over her itinerary for the *New Jersey Convention for Quality Food Products.*

A few boring lectures.

A promising speech on new FDA regulations.

Boring. More boring, boring, and meh.

But Toni had her mind flying right back to the core of all her woes. Of all the shitty things to happen to a girl, Annabeth had finally met her mate, only he didn't want her.

Irony of ironies—she'd been fated to a straight-faced, polite Shifter, who was currently acting as her chauffeur, and the motherfucker had turned her down.

Rejected.

There was just no other way to look at it. Though, to be fair, they'd both been kind of knocked over the head with the truth of their fated status. Uncle Uzzi had some serious explaining to do. But she wasn't mad at the older Witch.

Not really.

He couldn't be responsible for Hank's actions—*or lack thereof.*

Being one of four fiery Lioness sisters meant Annabeth was used to fighting for what she wanted. But how could she possibly put up a battle when he'd all but told her, sorry not interested?

ANNABETH

There is no Operation Claim the Cock, and could you be more vulgar?

She wanted to snap at her older sibling.

TONI

What do you mean? Oooh, you dirty kitty! I meant Cock as a euphemism for a male bird. But I see how it is. Speaking of which, have you seen it? And how is the old 🌶️🌶️🌶️ ? (Look, I found an eggplant emoji! —it means DICK!)

Annabeth was snorting with laughter at the several dozen eggplant emojis that filled her screen.

True, he'd stripped in order to shift in front of her Lioness last night, but the feline had been too preoccupied with his animal form to pay attention to certain male parts.

ANNABETH

Jury is out on the grounds of not having enough evidence.

TONI

Fine, party pooper. FYI, that's a no go on that elixir we talked about.

They need like a month at least to study your genetic makeup to come up with a solution. I had the lab send them samples, but it will take too long. Sorry, sweetie.

Well, crap. That sucked.

ADRIANNA

Just get him to boink you.

ARIELLA

For realz.

Okay, so her relationship with her sisters comprised of plenty of TMI and, over the top, banter. But, in her defense, the Golden girls had grown up with a pretty unusual mother. Patricia Golden was one hot mama. Not because widow set hearts on fire with lust whenever the sassy older woman was in the presence of the older Pride males.

Barf city.

Rather, Patricia was known as hot because of her mother's penchant for practical jokes, which she played mercilessly on the Pride. Such as the big s'mores cookout, which turned out to be even more fun when you added lighter fluid to everyone's individual tabletop fire pits.

Thank goodness Cousin Leon was a firefighter, Annabeth thought idly. But in all seriousness Patricia Golden loved her four girls, and one son— though George was a bit of an oddball, always preferring to stay on the outside of their wilder antics.

Their upbringing might not have been conventional, but theirs was a fierce and loyal kind of bond no one could break. And if someone tried, they best watch out cause the Goldens played rough.

Rawr!

"Everything alright?" Hank asked from the driver's seat, and she nodded her head and gave him a thumbs up.

Speech was a little impractical considering all the 🍆 🍆 🍆 still dancing across her screen, and the fact she was very, very interested in trying to recall what she'd seen in that photographic memory of hers.

Darn feline had been mesmerized by the way he'd grabbed his ankles, wings sprouting from his back, hands and feet morphing into two incredibly strong legs with wicked looking claws. She'd never seen anything like it.

Of course, her own Lioness was pretty dang awesome, if she said so herself. But his Gyrfalcon was a sight indeed. The spotted plumes of his feathers were regal looking and austere. As was the keen cobalt stare he'd given her before hopping onto the bed to share the space. Like it was their own little nest of blankets and pillows.

Sigh. If only.

Annabeth had done some quick-thinking last night to get through the uncomfortable situation of having to share a room with the male. Her heat was imminent, so much so, she'd even downed two more of the pills designed to stop a young feline's unwelcomed heat cycle from starting.

The fact the pills stopped working the older one got, did not mean she couldn't mess with the dosage, right? She still wasn't convinced she could keep her hands to herself, and that was why she'd decided on paws.

Swapping skin for fur, she'd been surprised at the sheer awe that practically saturated Hank's features as he took in her Lioness' form. Most felines suffered from a teeny-weeny problem with vanity. And while Annabeth was aware her inner kitty Cat was exceptional, it was still nice to be admired.

Especially by her mate.

Unmated mate, her Lioness huffed, annoyed at the little reminder.

ADRIANNA

Spill, girl.

She rejoined the chat, and Annabeth relented, filling in her other siblings, who'd joined the conversation, on the details of the night before.

ADRIANNA

Of course, he petted you. Lions are the best.

TONI

The trick is to get him to pet your other pussy.

ARIELLA

Girls, please, we aren't helping Annabeth here by being crude. Love, are you okay?

Her sudden insightfulness and sympathy made Annabeth's eyes burn with tears. Her sisters, despite the snark and mischief that went along with being a feline, were all remarkably close. And they loved each other fiercely. She could depend on them for support. No matter what.

ANNABETH

Look girls, the thing is, I know he is my mate. My animal picks him. But he made some promise to his parents before he met me, right before they died, to continue their line by only mating another Gyrfalcon.

He's explained it to me, but I just can't understand why his folks would make him promise something that would only hurt him. Maybe he just doesn't want me and doesn't want to be mean.

TONI

No fucking way.

ADRIANNA

The ass!

ARIELLA

Let's scalp him!

ANNABETH

NO!

ARIELLA

Spoilsport.

In fact, her quieter sister surprised Annabeth by adding a few knife emojis followed by birds, promising violence to the male.

TONI

I say we tar and feather the birdbrain. On top of his real feathers.

ARIELLA

So, that would be tar and feather his feathers, right?

ANNABETH

Girls, please!!! No hurting Hank!!!

TONI

Fine. If you say so. But we got your back, Anna-banana.

Sighing, Annabeth went back to the list of eligible males Toni had actually sent her. These Shifters would be at the convention, and as far as her sister knew, they were eligible bachelors.

Ugh.

She so did not want to go into her heat now, but what choice did she have?

"What's got you looking so serious back there?" Hank asked gently.

"Nothing," she said, shaking her head.

If only she could tell him the truth. Her she-Cat hissed and spat. The idea of bedding any other male had her shaking her leonine head firmly in the negative. The second she'd scented him, she knew he was the one for her.

Stupid male.

Why did he have to have principles? Sure, he'd

made the vow to his family when he was a kid, but the fact he was still trying to honor them meant he was a man who kept his promises. That was a good thing, right?

Unfortunately for her.

Annabeth scrolled through the list. It was slim pickings, as usual. Aside from Judd McCullen and Freddy Gennaro, there was Luca Bianco from Brooklyn. The man called himself the Cheese King, as if that were in some way appetizing. But the Bull Shifter did have the finest line of imported and organic cheeses Annabeth had ever tasted.

He was no Hank, but Luca had hinted the last time she'd seen him that he would be happy to plow her fields. The imagery had left her wanting. And not in the way the Bull had hoped.

Nope. No way.

In fact, it was quite the opposite. Annabeth had gone home alone after that event. Looked like this convention would end up with the same results if she somehow managed to stave off her heat.

For fuck's sake, Luca Bianco? The thought of the Bull Shifter slipping past her defenses made her ovaries want to shrivel up and die. And that would truly suck. Annabeth wanted cubs someday.

Or hatchlings. Fluffy little feathered ones.

Sad rawr.

A ping alerted her to the fact she'd gotten another PM. Annabeth really had to set some stronger boundaries with her sisters. *Sigh.*

UU

Annabeth, how are things going?

She paused. Reading and re-reading the missive until she realized who would be asking.

ANNABETH

Uncle Uzzi?

UU

Of course, it's me. Your mother gave me this address.

ANNABETH

I see, well, to be honest, I have a bone to pick with you.

UU

I know, dear, Hank emailed me last night. First, let me apologize for my nephew's unfortunate hardheadedness.

ANNABETH

I understand he made a vow to his dying father to mate a Gyrfalconess. Hank is just too good a son to go back on his word, Uncle Uzzi.

UU

Hank's father was an ass. But Hank has potential, Annabeth, I should know. I stayed in his life all these years, and there is no one who is more loyal or true than that man. The real question here is what exactly do you plan to do to snap him out of his misplaced notion that his bigoted parent should ruin his future?

Uncle Uzzi's answer stared at Annabeth for a moment, as if it were waiting for her response. She took a deep breath, then typed back.

ANNABETH

What? How can I change his mind? What are you saying exactly?

Her Lioness was already sitting up and ready to take notes from the world-famous matchmaker.

UU

Dear, didn't you ever read Shakespeare? The course of true love never doth run smooth.

ANNABETH

But Uncle Uzzi, he doesn't want me!

UU

Do you know that for sure? Have you tried seducing him?

Annabeth stared at the blinking cursor. Could Uncle Uzzi truly mean what she thought he meant? Only one way to find out.

ANNABETH

No! I mean, what do you mean?

She did not want to mess around or beat about the bush. This was Annabeth's future, for fuck's sake.

UU

Your sisters told me about last night, and while I applaud your quick wit, maybe you took the easy way out, Annabeth. Shifters are highly sexual creatures. You gotta let that cock crow, my dear.

The old Witch typed with the same no-nonsense attitude he was renowned for. And from the way the three little dots were blinking on the screen, he was not done.

UU

Annabeth, I am going to repeat a very old saying to you, and I hope you will get my meaning. Nothing ventured, nothing gained. You do know that if you want something, genuinely want it, sometimes you have to work for it. Do you really want Hank?

ANNABETH

Yes, Uncle Uzzi, I do. I really want him. My Lioness knows he is the one.

UU

Then what is the issue?

ANNABETH

Are you saying I should just pounce on him, and then what? Lick him until he surrenders?

In truth, her she-Cat was all for desperate measures. Her stomach cramped, a precursor to her heat, and she closed her eyes a moment. It was only Tuesday. By Friday, she would be a mess for sure.

UU

Lick him, kiss him, rub your booty on him. Whatever it takes. True love and happiness are worth the risk. Hank Garret is a good man. The best, really. I would not have introduced you otherwise. But he has a past, Annabeth.

ANNABETH

What do you mean?

She gnawed her lower lip while she waited, wanting to know anything she could about him.

UU

His parents were good people, but a little narrow-minded. Theirs was not a fated mating, Annabeth, and as such, their relationship was stilted. His home was not honest and warm like yours.

ANNABETH

That sucks, Uncle Uzzi, but my family is not perfect. We are loud and in your face most of the time.

She answered honestly. She knew instinctively Hank's reserve would temper her wilder impulses. In truth, she'd like the quiet meal they'd passed together.

UU

And it is wonderful, isn't it? Knowing your family accepts you regardless of any mistakes you might make. Hank's home life was cold. His parents did not believe in showing love or enthusiasm for anything their son did, and he did prove a little wild in a desperate attempt to gain their attention. That's when I started spending time with the young chick.

ANNABETH

That is so sad.

Her family's boisterous antics, and the absence of her father aside, she would never have gotten through her childhood without knowing her mom would be there for her with open arms, no matter what.

UU

Cold and lonely were the markers of his childhood and his parents' mating. Claudine was my friend, and I never believed she should have mated Hank's father, but her parents insisted. You see, like their wild cousins, Gyrfalcons return to the roost to propagate for generations dating back a thousand or more years. But that kind of tradition is nothing when pitted up against destiny.

ANNABETH

But he promised them.

UU

Oh, Annabeth, if he walks away and you let him, he will never have love or joy in his life. Is that what you think he should settle for?
Should you?

ANNABETH

It's not just up to me.

That was true, but Annabeth's Lioness pressed against her mind. The feline was angry at her for giving up without a fight.

Looked like Uncle Uzzi wasn't finished with her yet, as the three blinking dots would indicate. Annabeth inhaled. She had a feeling she would need her strength to read this next message.

UU

I guess, the real question here is are you a Lioness or a mouse?

ANNABETH

Uncle Uzzi, that's not fair.

UU

Life isn't fair, Annabeth. Now, I love Hank, and I think you do too. You know what to do. Let me know how it turns out. Good luck.

"Hungry?"

Annabeth jumped at the intrusion to her thoughts. Hank's eyebrows arched. His handsome face curious as he watched her in the rearview mirror.

Could I get away with it? With seducing him.

She wondered as her eyes flicked to Hank's cobalt gaze. He waited patiently for her response, though his expression was clearly befuddled.

She cleared her throat and nodded her head. Hungry? Yeah. Duh. She was Shifter. Of course, she was hungry. Hank exited the car walking to open her door, ever the consummate professional.

The ideal gentlemen to the core, isn't he? Maybe I can ruffle those perfectly coifed feathers of his after all, Annabeth thought with a predatory gleam in her golden eyes.

She took his proffered hand, though she didn't need it. Physical prowess was kind of a thing with dual-natured beings. But the contact, regardless of how slight, had her moaning internally.

Mmm.

It created the most delicious zing speeding through her blood. She was a Lioness, and never did things half-assed. Decision made, Annabeth held on, tugging his hand, and the rest of him closer as she slid out of the vehicle, making sure to brush against him with every inch of her body.

Hank sucked in a breath. A sound she longed to mimic. The feel of him, even through layers of clothing, was remarkable. But she forced herself to act nonchalant, releasing her hold and walking away.

She felt his stare. Heard the slight rumble in his chest. Knew he was not as immune as he pretended to be. Maybe her sisters and Uzzi, even her outrageous mother, were right. Sometimes you had to fight for what you wanted. And sometimes you had to fight dirty.

Annabeth had felt Hank's pulse racing during

their momentary embrace. She'd felt the hardness she'd conjured between his legs, noticed the flashes of jealousy and possessiveness he was not schooled enough to hide.

The man was fighting fate—theirs. And Annabeth was going to make it so much harder on him. She believed in happy ever afters and true love, but she also knew relationships required work and compromise. Sure, Hank made a promise, but according to Uzzi, it might not have been in his best interest.

Annabeth would never force him into anything. Not really. Her inner Lioness was positive he was hers. She felt all the things she'd heard about fated mates from the minute she'd seen him. Instant lust, possessive instincts, and more than that. Hank felt really important to her. He felt like air.

She'd seen him waver. Watched him convince himself it wasn't meant to be, but Annabeth didn't believe that. Yes, ultimately, it was both of their choices. But how would either of them know if they were meant for one another unless they tried?

Easy girl Everything is going to be purrfect, she thought, her inner feline sitting up and taking notes.

Hank Garret might think he was made for something else, but Annabeth could just about guarantee he was created just for her Lioness.

Time to test the feisty Falcon's resolve. And Annabeth knew just how to do it.

Rawrrrrr.

Chapter Eight

Holy. Fucking. Shit.

How could eating be sexy?

Oh—he thought as the little minx licked her spoon with her long, limber tongue —*that's how.*

Hank's eyes crossed for the umpteenth time as Annabeth ate her dessert with gusto. When he'd stopped for lunch at a promising looking burger joint, he had no idea the place was a throwback to the 1950s, complete with soda jerk and a long list of unusual homemade ice cream flavors.

Watching her eat had become something of an obsession for him. He worried about her comments regarding her shape. Crazy female. Didn't she know she was perfect?

Annabeth was not some dainty little miss. She was a motherfucking badass Lioness. A Hunter. A predator. A powerful, sexy, apparently brilliant, and cute as a button woman. She was funny, smart, ridiculously good at putting other people at ease. He'd watched her charm Rosa and Bob, and every sonovabitch waiter they'd had on their road trip—made longer by the unfortunate accident on the parkway.

But she was also honest and sweet. Her charm was natural, like those beautiful golden highlights in her hair. She was not like the usual business woman his company drove around. She looked at people when she spoke to them—and she never spoke never at them. That was particular pet peeve of his. Hank hated folks who put on airs. Funny, cause that is exactly what the entire flock of fuddy duddies at the North American Tower were like. They were nothing but a bunch of stuck up bird brains all caught up in breeding.

His Gyrfalcon growled and stretched his wings, clawing angrily at Hank's insides. The Tower had sent him an email that morning, and he'd yet to answer. His animal didn't want him to, but a promise was a promise. Right?

"Excuse me a minute, Hank, I need the little girl's

room," Annabeth interrupted his thoughts, and he nodded dumbly, pushing her plate and his to the center of the table.

They'd both ordered humongous triple beef patty burgers with buckets of cheddar cheese, mushrooms, onions, and a special sauce that had just a dab of horseradish, complete with a side of disco fries.

The luscious Lioness had practically jumped on the waiter when he'd suggested a frosty treat to finish the meal. The remnants of her strawberry sundae were melting in the bowl and Hank leaned forward to pluck on juice morsel from the side.

Delicious. Of course it was. His gaze roamed to find Annabeth walking back to their table. A stranger bumped into her, and Hank could tell the fucker had done it on purpose just to get his hands on her. He jumped up to intervene, but the saucy Lioness wasn't having that man's shit. She politely pushed the man's hands off her shoulders and nodded politely while walking away. Was it wrong that he felt so motherfucking proud of her?

Grrr. Hands off douches. This one is a badass.

Okay, so Hank sorta had an itty-bitty problem controlling his Falcon whenever she was out of his sight. Even now as she took her seat, the waiter came rushing over to offer a hand. Like she needed it. For fuck's sake.

"How was your sundae?" the kid asked.

"Are you kidding? It was amazing. Now, tell em you're eighteen cause a man who orders like you is just ripe for the marriage market, and honey, I am currently looking for a Mr. Golden," she joked.

Hank saw red as the young waiter blushed and flirted back with Annabeth. What. The. Fuck. She was proposing marriage to strangers now?

So what? It was just some harmless flirting.

Kak kak kak kak.

This was so not his business. And yet. He wasn't so sure about that since his talons were threatening to pop out when the young male cocked his hip to the side and gave Annabeth a slow once over.

"I'm nineteen, Miss. Plenty old enough," the young server replied.

"I bet you drive all the girls crazy," Annabeth complimented him as she handed over her credit card.

Fuck. When did she sneak that past him?

"I would have paid," he grumbled.

"It's fine," she replied coolly, looking down at her phone.

It was a Shifter run place, most every restaurant

or hotel on his radar was. Hank preferred that to places where normals frequented whenever he was *enroute* with a client.

But Annabeth is not just a client, is she?

Shut. The. Fuck. Up.

He snarled at his raptor, shushing the animal.

Hank did not want to hear any more about it. Bad enough he was doomed to be in her presence for another half hour.

Okay, he relented.

Doomed was a harsh word. Being with Annabeth was not exactly a hardship. She was fun and gorgeous, a true pleasure to be with. In fact, he could not quite wrap his head around the fact he would not see her after this.

Shit. That felt wrong. He was going to miss her. Her smile, her laughs, her quick wit, and sense of humor. The way she tapped along in time with whatever music she'd turned on when they were driving. The way she ate ice cream.

Holy fuck.

Those lips, that tongue, her whimpers of pleasure all brought to mind dirtier, naughtier things he'd like to do to elicit such erotic sounds from her tempting mouth.

Sigh.

He really had to stop this. Driving with a hard on was fucking difficult. Driving with the worst case of blue balls he'd ever had in his life was damn near impossible.

Want. Claim. Mark.

Hank was Falcon enough to admit he wanted the sultry little morsel, but he was not claiming or marking anyone. He'd made a promise, and he felt obligated to keep it.

Break the fucking promise. She is ours.

"Excuse me. I'll be right back," he murmured.

He needed to splash some cold water on his face before he got in the car again. His father's words came back to him as he stood up to use the washroom.

"Hank, real men honor their vows. They respect tradition. You must keep to the family ways. Stay with your own and ensure our survival."

As a kid, he'd hated his stern father's lessons and warnings. The man was never happy, and it showed. He did not even seem to like his only son. Hated it when he'd tried to make friends with other Shifters at school.

"Stay away from the riffraff, Hank. They are not our kind."

He'd kept the young *eyas* homeschooled and

away from others. But that only served to enhance the boy's curiosity. In fact, now that he thought about it. His father had controlled a lot of Hank's and his mother's social lives.

They'd never attended community functions, only those of the Tower. Traveling great distances to visit with other Falcon families whom the great Gerald Garret thought worthy of receiving them. Shifters with old money, their circle of friends, or whatever you wanted to call them, were small.

Those days sucked, his Gyrfalcon reminded him.

That is why we started the Falcon Limousine Service. All Shifters. No holds barred. Remember our fledgling years? No friends. No smiles. It was bad, Hank.

Annabeth smiles. She makes us smile.

Hank's eyes darted back to where Annabeth sat in the booth, licking the last bit of chocolate hazelnut strawberry ice cream from her spoon. Her golden eyes closed as she savored the mouthful, and he wished he were sitting beside her, kissing that dribble of chocolate from the corner of her mouth.

The server, who'd remained to chat with the lovely feline, lifted a napkin and wiped the spot, causing an inordinate amount of jealousy to rise, and swiftly too. It was so intense, it damn near strangled him.

Hank growled low in his throat. The sound easily deciphered by the Shifters in the joint. The waiter looked up. Eyes wide, he yanked on the collar of his shirt, then excused himself quickly while Hank walked back to the booth.

He took the spoon from Annabeth's suddenly lax hand, realizing a little belatedly that she was staring at him with her mouth open. Okay, so his behavior was sort of shocking. But what was a guy to do? He tossed a few bills on the table, paying the tip before she could add it to the receipt, and grabbed her hand.

Hank yanked her up none too gently, but that was okay. She was Lioness, and he was holding onto his skin by a thread. The young waiter's scent lingered around her, and that really pissed him off. He moved closer behind her, hands on her waist and proceeded to frog-march the naughty kitten out the door, straight to his limousine.

"What the heck, Hank? I wasn't done—"

"You were finished," he growled, clicking the key fob to unlock the doors before he gently shoved her inside.

"What are you doing?"

Too late, he realized he'd followed her into the spacious backseat of the Rolls. Chest heaving, Hank was hardly thinking straight. How could he when she was barely decent?

His keen eyes roamed over her long, silky legs. Both were fully exposed in the frilly little sundress she'd donned that morning. The pretty thing rode up to her panty line when she'd moved over to give him room. He was having a hard time seeing anything except the miles of skin revealed.

"Hank," she said and snapped her fingers in front of him. "What do you think you're doing?"

"I don't know," he growled in answer to her question.

It was the truth. He had no idea what he was doing. He was shaking from head to toe, his animal on edge. Fuck. He was so mixed up. She was so damn close. So beautiful. And yet so far out of his reach.

"I don't know what to do, Annabeth," he confessed, and for the first time in his life, he allowed someone else to see his vulnerability.

Would she hate him now? Think of him as weak?

He should have known better. Annabeth took the decision out of his hands. One second, she was sitting beside him, the next she was astride him. Every inch of her luscious body pressed against his, and Hank's Falcon screamed in victory inside his head.

Her hands cupped his face—warm, strong, yet gentle hands. He could hardly breathe. She smiled then, pulling him closer until his lips were at just the right angle to be seized by hers.

Holy fuck.

The second her lips touched his, it was as if he'd been hit by lightning. Like a hundred thousand bolts of lightning. That zap that would have killed a lesser man. But the charge only made his cock harder than ever before.

Heat seeped through his pants, bathing his dick in warmth from her cleft, which was at the moment pressed snug against him. He settled his hands on her buttocks, the soft globes bared to him beneath her skirt.

Oh shit.

She wore a pair of sexy silk cheekster panties. A discovery he made while tracing the seam of the fabric along the crack of her sumptuous ass. Annabeth moaned, rocking against him as his tongue invaded her mouth.

She was sweet, so sweet, he was about to go into a diabetic coma. And he would, gladly too, just to have her. Her strawberry-flavored essence was too good to waste a single drop on self-doubt or moderation. Hell no, he was too greedy for her to give her up. Not then. Maybe not ever.

Yes. Mark. Claim. Bite.

His Gyrfalcon screeched mightily as her hands scratched at his shoulders through his shirt.

No. No marking, no claiming.

But still, he could enjoy a small taste, couldn't he? Without breaking his vow.

"Yes," murmured Annabeth.

Her hands were caught between them, and he realized she was working the buttons of his shirt open. Hank hissed out a breath as she raked her nails down his chest, moving to his belt buckle.

"Fuck," he growled when her lips left his, going for a nibble of his chest and nipple.

"We have to stop, Annabeth."

The *kak kak kak* of his Gyrfalcon echoed in his brain, almost deafeningly so. Annabeth paid him no heed.

Thank fuck.

He bucked in response to her ministrations. The soft suction of her warm mouth felt so good on his nipples, and lower as she worked the buckle to his trousers open. He could not move, could not breathe, or think for that matter as cool air hit his newly freed cock.

Annabeth slid to her knees on the floor of the spacious limousine and had him in her mouth before he could utter a single protest.

Lick, suck, slurp, and repeat.

"Fuck," he growled, hips flexing in time with her marvelous ministrations,

Hank gripped her by the hair, unusually vocal as the gorgeous female bobbed her head up and down along his shaft. Her hands reached down to cup his balls, squeezing and fondling.

Her touch was like magic. Nothing had ever felt so perfect. Fuck, she looked gorgeous, taking him deep and moaning along his shaft. Hank bellowed as he came, and the naughty little minx milked him of every drop, swallowing his cum as if he were something delicious.

Sexy, beautiful, fierce Lioness. Badass kitty.

"Mmm," she grinned like the naughty kitten she was. "Now that is what I call dessert."

She moved to the other side of the limo, but Hank didn't let her go too far. Hands gripping her luscious hips, he pressed her down into the seat, inserting himself between her creamy thighs.

"My turn," he growled. "Kittens aren't the only ones who like cream."

Golden eyes glowed as Annabeth gasped, watching him shove the cotton dress up to her waist. He ran his fingertips along the damp silk panties, taking his time to slowly circle her swollen bud.

"So wet for me," he growled.

"Hank," she breathed his name, mouth parted, panting for breath as he lowered his head.

"Your scent is so delicious, kitten," he replied huskily and closed his mouth over her silk-covered mound, suckling her through the scrap of fabric.

"Mine."

The word slipped out of its own volition. But Hank did not stop to wonder. He simply nudged the silk aside, his entire body tense as he gazed upon the short-cropped, gold curls that covered her sex.

Annabeth moaned out loud with the first swipe of his tongue. Hands fisting his hair, he didn't even care that she mussed his stylish do as he feasted on her delectable goodies.

His right hand reached for the plump mounds he'd been fantasizing about for the last twenty-four hours. So soft, so perfect. Annabeth was a goddess put here to torment him, of that one fact, he was certain.

The elasticized top gave way, allowing for easy access, and once more he said a fervent thank you to whoever designed this dream of a dress. She was so pretty in it. Better without it, he could only guess. Little flowers danced across the fabric, bursting with energy, joy, and life. Much like his naughty little kitten.

He might not be ready to admit it yet, but Hank had never felt such sweet bliss as he did right then. Giving into the temptation to rock her world, he closed his mouth over her needy clit, sucking hard and relishing the tug of her hands and the sound of her gasps.

With her puckered nipple caught in his hand, Hank tugged and squeezed, sucking her the whole time. Then, as if he knew she needed something more, just a little bit extra to push her over the edge, Hank growled, using the vibration to send her rocketing into bliss.

Good thing he was there to catch her.

His sweet Lioness did not come quietly. Oh no, head tossed back, she rocked her hips against his mouth, tugging him closer by his hair. And fuck if he didn't love it. A knock on the window brought his head up. The snarl that ripped through the air, however, did not belong to him.

It was hers. The sound shot straight to his cock, and he fought the urge to ignore the idiot on the other side of the door and bury himself in her heat.

"Just a sec, lover, I'll get rid of this jerk. By the way, do you have a shovel?" she asked.

It was all he could do to stop her from moving, but he managed it. With a firm command to stay, Hank pressed a hot, desperate kiss on her lips, then turned to the window. He lowered it just a fraction to see the pasty-faced waiter standing there nervously.

"You, uh, forgot your credit card, Miss," the waiter's voice cracked as he held a trembling hand with Annabeth's credit card through the window.

The kid yelped when Hank grabbed it with semi-formed talons on the end of his hands. Body still on fire with need, clarity came suddenly when he realized what they'd been doing.

"You didn't have to scare the poor kid," Annabeth said, and even without turning around, he could hear the smile in her voice.

She seemed to like the wildly possessive streak that in all honesty scared the bejesus out of him. Hank had never expected to feel such emotions before.

Jealousy? Him? Nah.

But there it was again when she glanced out the window to wave at the *for-some-unknown-reason-likely-to-get-him-maimed-still-standing-there-waiter.* Hank snarled and closed the window.

"Uh," he cleared his throat. "We have a little while before we get there. Better buckle up."

Then he was moving back to his seat behind the wheel. He felt Annabeth's confusion pressing down on him, but what was he supposed to do about it?

"I think we should get to know each other better," she announced brightly.

"I don't think that is a good idea."

"Why not? We already started," she said and smirked.

"Annabeth, please don't mistake what just happened for anything permanent," he started.

But she wasn't listening. Actually, that was an understatement. Annabeth was already climbing over and through the currently rolled down partition that would otherwise separate him from his clients.

"Why not?" she asked, wide smile in place.

He tried not to glance at the pretty post-orgasmic flush that pinkened her cheeks and left her gold eyes sparkling in the late afternoon sunshine. But shit, it was too late.

She was gorgeous, and he was an idiot if he thought he was going to get away unscathed. This feline had the power to completely turn his life upside down.

The question was—did Hank want that?

Yessss.

Chapter Nine

After another round of twenty questions, Annabeth was no closer to breaking through the tough exterior that Hank had shown her time and again.

It was impenetrable. The force field around his heart was so thick and strong she'd bet the current owners of the *Millennium Falcon* would love to get the schematics for their spacecraft. Even after she left the spacious backseat to sit beside him in the front of the Phantom, she couldn't seem to ruffle the man's impeccable feathers.

Sad rawr.

"How far are we?"

"We just entered Atlantic City a few minutes ago.

There's always some traffic in town, but we shouldn't be too long," he said.

Was it her imagination, or did the steely-eyed Falcon sound sad? She watched carefully for any sign that he was feeling something, anything, but nope. He gave nothing away. Eyes on the road, he barely glanced at her.

Discouraging? Yep.

Her phone chirped, and she glanced down to see a text from her boss looking for an update. Crap. Annabeth had almost forgotten this was a working trip.

"Excuse me, I have to take this," she said, and scrounged behind her for her laptop.

She felt her skirt fly up in the wake of the air conditioner he'd put on at her request, but she was not concerned. Hank's face had been plastered to her pussy mere minutes ago. It wasn't anything he hadn't seen.

Of course, the rumbling sound coming from him said otherwise. She blushed as she snagged the computer and turned back around.

"You know, you should wear full briefs with a dress," he murmured.

"Why? Cause I'm chubby? Contrary to popular belief, girls with fat asses happen to like the comfort of butt-less panties regardless of their attire," she replied with a huff.

Now that her happy after sexy times feelings had gone away, Annabeth was a little raw. Hank was a tough nut to crack. He was denying them a chance at real happiness and for no reason at all.

The screech of the tires almost sent her flying forward, but Shifter reflexes had her bracing herself as he skidded to a stop on the side of the road.

"Look at me," he growled in a deep voice she hardly recognized.

"What?" she snapped.

"Annabeth, you may be wild, and a little unconventional, but there is absolutely nothing fat about you."

"What?" she repeated, only quieter.

Speechless was not something anyone had ever rendered her before, and yet, there she was. So quiet she could hear every thud of her heart in her chest with glaring accuracy.

First time for everything.

Her Lioness preened at his ready praise. In fact, Annabeth's tongue practically lolled out of her head as he continued.

"You. Are. Perfect. From the top of your golden

head to the soles of your gorgeous size tens," Hank said, fingers gripping her chin gently as he talked.

Then, the sexy man winked, sending tendrils of happiness shooting through her. He thought she was perfect. Was it possible to turn into a puddle of goo? Annabeth's insides were already a melty pot of mushiness from his praise.

Sweet, tempting, sexy man.

"Thanks," she replied demurely.

What the fuck? Lionesses did not demure. Like ever.

Annabeth shook her head and opened her tablet, prepared to do some work until they arrived at the hotel for the convention. She was bound by the EWLP contract to inform her boss of her impending heat, as it might render her unable to attend the main event. Afterwards, she could check her itinerary, and shoot off a PM to her sisters.

Annabeth could not help herself. She'd found a gif of a huge dancing eggplant. One press of her fingers and the message was delivered followed by the sound of a dozen chimes and hearts emojis from the girls.

LOL.

A little while later, Hank rolled to a stop in front of the newest location on the east coast of *Stein*

Luxury Resorts & Hotels, known as *Jersey Gardens*. The place was gorgeous.

All modern lines, clean glass, steel, and brick. It looked clean, sophisticated, and yet inviting, with the wide spaces and access to the pine barrens just behind it. Annabeth had to bite back her moan of disappointment. Hank had truly made it there in record time. And now he was going to leave. So much for vamping him.

Very sad rawr.

Her stomach tightened, clenching uncomfortably. Annabeth took an elastic band out of her purse and swept her hair back, away from her face. She blinked her eyes.

Fuck, was this nausea because they were about to part forever? Crap. Annabeth felt sick. She ignored her momentary discomfiture and exited the vehicle. His face was devoid of expression as he gathered her things and loaded the trolley, walking her inside while she checked in to the establishment.

She felt hollow all of a sudden. Their tempestuous exchange had been so hot, so intense. Like shooting stars colliding. Maybe Uncle Uzzi was wrong about them being fated mates. Annabeth's heart squeezed painfully. Maybe they really were shooting stars on a collision course. So damned hot when they'd collided together, but temporary. So very temporary.

The thought left her empty and so damn sad she couldn't breathe. Annabeth was sweating despite the cool air coming from the gilt air-conditioning vent in the ritzy wall of the lobby. Her stomach cramped, and her Lioness hissed.

"Oh no," Annabeth murmured, eyes going wide.

"What is it?" Hank asked, appearing beside her while she dug in her purse for her heat cycle suppressants.

"I'm all out. Fuck," she whispered.

Beneath her clothing, Annabeth felt her breasts swell with needy pangs of arousal that were all part and parcel of a feline's heat. Her sex throbbed. Stomach ached. And dammit, she was so warm.

No. No. NO!

Soon, the need to be filled by the next available dick would hurt, and not just like an itch or an ache. Annabeth would feel real, unbearable pain if she did not find someone to pass her cycle with. Fear spiked through her. She hated being at the mercy of her biological needs.

Evolution be damned. Shifters were rare and secret from the human world, and this little fucked up quirk somehow ensured their survival. But it was not fair.

"Annabeth?"

"I have to get out of here," she whimpered.

Annabeth would soon be desperate for a male to ease her. Any male. The thought revolted her. Especially now that she'd met her mate.

"What can I do?"

"Just get me to my room," she growled low in her voice, still searching her purse.

"What are you looking for?" Hank asked.

"My suppressants. They don't work like they used to. I guess I've been taking too many at once, and now I am out."

"Are you sure? Let me check your suitcase," Hank said and walked her down the hall to the elevator.

He seemed attuned to her rising anxiety, patting the outside zippers of her bag, oblivious to the Shifter who got on at the next floor. Annabeth only wished she could say the same. She smiled tensely, but she saw his nostrils flare and saw the heat in his gaze. It made her sick.

"Hello, Ms. Golden," Luca Bianca sided up to her, he took her hands with both of his leaned in and kissed her on either cheek, inhaling deeply.

"It is so nice to see you. You know your mother

called my father, told him about your little problem. I was just on my way to the lobby to see if you checked in yet," he said, eyeing her up and down like she was a cookie and he some chubby schoolboy.

All she wanted was to push his grimy hands off her and walk away. But considering they were stuck in an elevator, where could she go?

"I'd like to offer you my services," the creep said.

Revulsion filled her, but another wave of cramping hit. Being a female really sucked sometimes. Gritting her teeth against the nasty words she so wanted to shout at the cretin, Annabeth managed a weak smile. Luca was a jerk, but he was not bad to look at. A little conceited, but most males were.

She only wanted Hank. But he had already rejected her. Her Lioness yowled, the feline demanding she take her mate. She couldn't even look at him, though she was aware he'd stopped moving. Just remained crouched on the floor, hands on her suitcase.

It was time she faced facts. The interlude in the Phantom had been everything, but it was not enough. It was not a claim.

Hank. Did. Not. Want. Her. For. Keeps.

The truth hurt, but Annabeth did not think she

could settle for less. With her heart heavy, she turned to Luca's seedy smile.

"Actually, I might need," she began, panting with the effort it was taking to stand there and talk, but Hank's low growl interrupted her.

"Unless you want to permanently lose the use of those hands, get the fuck off her," snarled Hank, before he slowly stood up from his position on the floor, rolling to his feet with more grace than any of the Big Cat species she'd ever seen.

Shit. Was he always so tall? So wide?

He looked fucking enormous, and mad as a hornet as he bared his teeth and puffed his chest. Annabeth just stared at him. He was usually so composed, but now, her mouth hung open as he fisted the collar of Luca's shirt, lifting the big man clear off the floor.

For a Falcon, he sure was strong. The elevator doors opened, and Hank sent poor, shocked Luca flying over the tiled floor. He leaned over and pushed the closed button, jaw clenched so tight, she wondered if he broke any teeth.

Yes. Strong. Good mate.

"Um, Hank—"

"Don't. Say. A. Word," he growled. "Not yet."

She watched him warily. One hand on her lower

stomach as another wave of heat pulsed through her. Dammit. Her sex ached. Annabeth squeezed her legs together to relieve some pressure, but it did not help. She felt Hank stir beside her, heard him sniffing the air and clicking his tongue behind his teeth in that habit he had when he was incensed.

"I know this makes me a total asshole, Annabeth," he began, "and I will readily admit it to the whole fucking world. But I won't let him have you. I can't. If it has to be someone, it will be me. Okay?"

Unable to speak, she nodded fervently. Her Lioness had already decided. She'd been stuck on him since she first laid eyes on the striking male.

"Let's go."

Hank took her hand and pulled her along the corridor until he located her room. Shoving the bags carelessly against the wall, Hank lifted her up princess-style, and carried her inside.

Strong, sweet, fairytale hero.

A wave of need speared her like a knife, and she cried out with it. The ache was sharp and precise. Like a wave of sexual energy that had just eclipsed into tsunami proportions. Her sex moistened, and Annabeth turned sparkling gold eyes on him.

"Hank, you don't have to do this," she said,

shaking her head, knowing full well he didn't want to.

Oh, he wanted to have sex with her. But he did not want her for keeps. With anyone else, she would go through the motions, but with him, Annabeth did not know if she could survive what came next. She did not know if she could take him leaving her.

"Shhh," Hank whispered, pressing kisses to her face as another wave of lust hit her, hard. "I want to. I need to, Annabeth."

Heat cycles differed from feline to feline. For Annabeth, who had been avoiding the full-blown biological occurrence until she'd found her mate, it was that much more intense.

Her scent thickened, arousal increasing her natural musk, and she wondered briefly if he would be affected by it. She pressed her legs together, scissoring her thighs trying to relieve the ache. Shocked by how quickly it had progressed, she moaned and kicked off her shoes.

"I can't. My clothes. I'm sorry. Feel too hot. Too tight," she groaned.

Mate. Bite. Claim.

Annabeth shook her head against her Lioness' train of thought. Typically fated mates would be on each other like mad, but what if his response was merely biological?

No. She could not mate him. Annabeth would not risk it. Yes, she wanted him, but she was not about to tie herself to him blindly.

"Let me help, Annabeth. Can I?" Hank asked, stilling his actions as he sought to undress her to relieve some of the pressure.

"Please. But no biting, Hank. Just sex."

His blue eyes burned into her soul as he gritted his teeth. She felt her heat burning at full blast, but if he did not agree, Annabeth would ask him to leave. She would rather spend the night locked in the bathroom writhing in pain than have him mate her without his consent.

"Okay. Sex only. No claim marks," he growled his reply, and his voice went impossibly deep.

"It burns," she groaned and gasped as her clothes became unbearable.

Hank growled, hovering above her. He reared up, hands on the collar of her dress, then he flicked his blue gaze at her face and ripped. Annabeth had never had this happen before. Oh, she'd torn clothing in a frenzy or haste, but it had mostly been her clumsy ministrations that led to it.

When Hank tore her dress away with his talon-tipped hands, he looked fierce and powerful, and oh so fucking hot. She moaned when he ran his hands down her now naked body, uncaring that the lights were on and he was seeing all her jiggly bits.

"I got you," he growled, nuzzling her legs apart and inserting his own between them while he crashed his lips to hers.

He worked on his clothes next, all the while kissing her and stroking her with his lips. Fuck, the man could kiss. Annabeth moaned against his seeking tongue. The wonderful appendage stroked along hers, tangling and wrestling for dominance while he petted and caressed every inch of her, smoothing away their underthings expertly until they were both gloriously bare.

Lucky for them, Stein Luxury Resorts were owned by supernaturals. That meant the furniture was sturdy, and each room was soundproofed. Doubly so. Otherwise, who knew what folks would think with all the kak kak kaking, purring, and growling going on in her suite?

Sexy man. Good kisser. Lover.

Annabeth hissed in anticipation as Hank pressed her down on the bed before lifting off. He stood, butt naked and gorgeous, the hard muscles of his abs flexed as he looked at her with appreciation in his gaze that she reciprocated, looking her fill at his muscled body.

Her eyes worshipped him as he revealed his thick biceps, swollen pecs, and rippling abdominals. She'd done some reading on their road trip, and even in the wild Gyrfalcons were thought of as stocky, muscular predators. With all the speed and deadly efficiency of other raptors, this man was the largest and most deadly of the group.

The stuff that made ancient Egyptians use the head of a falcon to represent their god, Horus. She could understand why they would want to worship the raptor as a cosmic entity whose body delineated the heavens.

Holy smokes, his body sure is heavenly.

Cobalt blue eyes flashed as he lowered himself, kissing his way down her blushing body. Annabeth hissed. Her Lioness with her every step of the way. Each touch, every slide of his skin against hers, every nibble and peck—*all of it*—was magnified tenfold in her heat.

And they'd only just begun.

The sun and the moon shone in his eyes as he speared her with his reverent gaze, and she nearly lost her grip on reality as his callused fingers traced the swollen lips of her sex before he dipped down for an open-mouthed kiss.

"Fuck me," she whimpered.

As if her words egged him on, Hank began to eat her in earnest, creating fires in her belly as he brought her to the edge of oblivion and back again. Teasing, seducing, making her wild with need.

"Feels so good," Annabeth groaned as he licked her from her dripping cleft to her throbbing clit.

"Yesssss, I am going to fuck you. Gonna make sure you feel good everywhere," he hissed, going down for another swipe.

Moisture pooled from her sex, and Annabeth screamed in delight as he pushed blunted fingers into her tight sheath.

"So tight," he growled.

If sensations could be labeled and put in order alphabetically, Annabeth could have worked her way down the list. Sure, that she felt each and every one of them while Hank feasted on her so fabulously.

Astonished. Bewildered. Crazed. Decadent. Excited. Flustered. Greedy. Hot. Infatuated. Joyful. Keen. Lusty. Magical. Needy. Orgasmic. Passionate. Quaking. Rapturous. Satisfied. Tender. Unbelievable. Vibrant. Wonderful. Xenial. Yowling. Zealous.

Fuck yes. All that and more. So much more.

For the first time in her life, Annabeth felt fulfilled. Hank was more than determined to bring her pleasure amidst her heat, and she was so fucking grateful, she vibrated with it.

Oh wait. That was him, she moaned as he rumbled with his mouth latched onto her clit.

The rumbling pleasure as he swapped fingers and tongue was so intense, she thought she would die from it. His tongue pierced her channel while he used his thumbs to rub her bundle of nerves in titillating circles.

"More," she moaned, pumping her hips in time with his thrusts.

So close. Close. CLOSE.

Mindless to everything else around her, Annabeth focused on the careful attentions of Hank's expert mouth. He was so goddamned good, filling her so deeply with his tongue. He ate her like a starving man at his first meal in months.

"NOW!" she yelled, pulling on his hair as he *lick, lick, licked* her to fruition.

Her orgasm raced over her like a steamroller with a jet engine. She yanked on his hair again, pulling him off her sex. She needed more from him, and he went willingly. Licking a path from her pussy to her mouth, Annabeth welcomed the taste of her own desire on his lips, while searching for his cock with her hands.

Once she had him, Annabeth fixed him with her stare. He pulsed in her hand, so swollen and hard. Like eleven inches of warm stone wrapped in velvet.

Yummy.

"Are you sure about this, Hank? I know I am in heat, and you are reacting to that. I know you have other plans for your future, but I need you to be okay with this. I won't make any permanent bonds between us. No biting. No claiming. I need you, but I won't take you if you don't want to be here."

"Does it feel like I don't want you, Annabeth?" he asked, flexing his hips so his hard cock inched closer to her entrance.

"I need you, Hank," she whimpered as his lips skimmed hers.

"I want you, Annabeth," he said, and fuck, that felt important.

"Just this. Just now. Okay?"

Annabeth could not allow his words to mean more than what they did. He wanted her. Now. Just for now.

Being in the middle of a heat cycle was dangerous for females. Many a cousin had regaled her with horror stories of *claimings* that had taken place during the rough, marathon sex that often accompanied a Shifter's heat.

Annabeth knew Hank was hers. But she could not allow him to tie himself to her because of biology. That would never be enough for her. And she would not allow him to settle for that either. If they mated under these circumstances, he'd resent her in time. Annabeth could not live with herself if that happened.

"Annabeth," he growled, flexing his hips.

"Want you. Need you, sweet. Lemme have you," he begged, and fuck, that felt good too.

"I need you too," she confessed between his expert caresses and kisses.

"No promises. Just sex," she repeated, more for herself than for him.

She was hardly lucid, but she needed to remember that very important thing. Hank was not hers for keeps. After this, he was going to walk away, and Annabeth was going to have to move on with her life.

"No more thinking, kitten. Just feel," he growled against her lips.

His cock throbbed in her hand, and her sex was so needy for him. Her Lioness snarled and snapped her massive jaws.

Claim him already, but she ignored the feline and focused on her lover.

"Last chance to back out," she offered, removing her hold on his cock.

She moaned as his mushroomed head breached her entrance, holding his blue gaze with hers.

"I've never been more certain of anything in my life," he said, his gravelly voice stroked her as sure as his thick shaft.

Then she was gasping, clutching his shoulders as he pressed his hips forward and sunk balls deep into her hot pussy. Annabeth purred as his girthy length seemed to touch every significant part of her core.

"Fuck, kitten," Hank grunted as he withdrew, then pushed inside. He did it again, and again in fast, hard drives that left her panting.

"You feel so fucking perfect," he growled the words through clenched teeth.

Annabeth had to agree. She was no virgin, but sex was on a whole new level when it was with her mate.

Mark him.

No!

She pushed the she-Cat back down as he pounded into her. Who knew her Falcon liked to talk so dirty? The things he whispered. Praising her bountiful curves, describing the feel of her slick sheath fisting his cock as he slid in and out, brought her unexpected pleasure.

"S'tight/ S'hot. You like my cock buried inside of you, kitten? Gonna get you off so good," he promised.

And fuck yes, he already was. Her nerve endings were already buzzing with promises of her next orgasm when he turned it up another notch.

Pulling out of her wanting sex, he flipped her over, and she sighed. Thankfully, he was not finished yet. Hands pressed her back down into the mattress, Hank lifted her ass up high, spreading her thick thighs.

"S'gorgeous," he grunted, rubbing his fingers over her engorged clit.

"Ohh," she stammered, unable to find the right words.

Then it was only sensation after sensation as he worshipped her reverently with his hands, mouth, and tongue. No one had ever made her feel small and cherished, sexy and bold, wanted and needed, all at the same time. No one but Hank.

Desperate and wanting the release she instinctively knew he could bring, Annabeth moaned. His lips, his hands, all touched her in a million places at once. It was almost too much, but still not enough.

"Please," she begged, but she didn't have to for long.

No sooner had he removed his hands, then he was filling her again. Splitting her open on his cock, that seemed even bigger than before. His fingers gripped her hips tightly, almost painfully, as he fucked her from behind.

Dropping forward, Hank caged her in. Their sweat-slicked bodies gliding against one another as he cupped her breasts with one hand, tweaking the nipples and tugging them in time with his thrusts.

"I'll take care of you," he grunted.

"Hank," she moaned his name as another wave of pleasure eclipsed over her.

"Beautiful. So fucking beautiful, Annabeth. Feel s'good."

No one had ever spoken to her like that during sex. She'd never been described like some sexy goddess he couldn't wait to have again. Even as they loomed on the precipice, he whispered to her, until he could no longer speak.

And wasn't that sexy as fuck?

It wasn't long before he joined her, tipping her over the edge on her third orgasm so far. Coming simultaneously, Annabeth could hardly breathe as he flexed his hips, spilling hot cum into her womb and marking her with his scent.

If she could not have his bite, at least she would have this, she thought as her pussy contracted around him, milking him of every last drop.

Mine, her she-Cat said determinedly.

Not yet. But maybe.

No one could blame her for dreaming.

Chapter Ten

Hank was in a haze of sex and lust. Holy hell. Annabeth had gone into her heat almost immediately upon their arrival at the hotel.

Not ten minutes inside and the scent of her pheromones almost knocked him out with their intensity. But it was more than just a gut reaction. His bird wanted to protect her, to help her, to cherish her.

Thank fuck they were in the elevator. He'd been so preoccupied trying to find her pills to ease her pain, he hardly realized they'd picked up a passenger until the fucker had touched his sweet little Lioness.

Hank had almost lost his fucking mind when that

creepy cheese peddler put his slimy hands on his woman.

Mine, screeched his Falcon.

Not for the first time since he'd met her, he readily agreed with the pesky bird of prey. The curvy goddess of a Lioness was a handful, but he had to admit, she was a delight. Smart as a whip, friendly, funny, and fierce when need be. She stirred his mind, and his passions, and she made him happy.

As in, he hadn't stopped smiling since he practically carried her to her hotel suite forty-eight hours ago. Two days of nonstop sexy fun times, and Hank was addicted as fuck.

He'd unwrapped the woman like a present. Kissed every inch of her sweet flesh. Damn near lost his mind when he rolled her onto her belly and caught a glimpse of the tiny tattoo that graced her left butt cheek.

"A falcon?" he asked later, in a raspy voice hoarse from growling and crying out in their passionate exchange.

She'd nodded her head, blushing prettily.

"I was always a fan of the falconer at the Ren Faire. The birds of prey show was my favorite when I was a cub. One time, a falcon swooped down and sat on my shoulder.

The man was surprised, said he never did that. I fell in love with that animal. Do you like it?" she'd asked.

"Depends. Who gave it to you? I need his name and number so I can tear the fucker's eyes out."

"Toni," she'd laughed out loud, obviously not caring if he killed the SOB.

"Where does Tony live?"

"Toni with an i. She's my sister," she'd added, and he exhaled.

Truth was, he did like the sassy bit of ink. Quite a lot, actually. And he proceeded to show her by petting and kissing the feathered ink rendition that decorated her silky-smooth skin until they were both going at it full speed ahead.

Every inch of Annabeth was beautiful. And he showed her. Let her know with the way he'd worshiped at her altar. He could've spent months between her thighs, feasting on her, stamping himself over every inch of her.

The strawberry flavored musk that was all her invaded his senses. It wrapped around him like a blanket, but instead of overheating him, it created the perfect nest. A cocoon of desire and longing he never wanted to leave.

Hank had never assisted a Shifter in heat before. Bird Shifters did not experience that kind of thing far as he knew. Besides, he usually dated humans. But the second he'd felt Annabeth's biological clock go at it, his dick stood up at attention. Raring to go was another way to describe his state.

Even after their two-day fuck-a-thon, he was insatiable. This was more than hormones and biology. Annabeth's strawberry flavored musk, now combined with his own breezy scent, was imprinted on his skin, his tongue, his fucking brain. Still, he craved her.

The sweet Lioness snuggled into his side. Poor thing was exhausted. Emotion washed over him, and the need to take care of her, not just now but for always, raised to levels he had no idea existed inside of him.

Who knew a heat cycle could be so demanding?

Trays littered the corner of the suite. They'd ordered in every meal, but he knew his sweet kitten would be starved when she woke up. He'd already placed their next order and was waiting for it to arrive, even now. With the sun peeking through the curtains, he gauged the time to be around noon. Any minute now, the hotel waitstaff would come knocking on the door, leaving a cart with the day's selections.

He nuzzled her neck, loving the way she opened

for him, and cursed her lack of mating mark. He'd wanted so many times to make her his own, but she'd insisted. Hell, he thought for sure she would relent, but not his stubborn little kitten.

Once or twice, he might have tried to gain the upper hand, to force his mark on her, but she was no pushover. Any wrestling matches that flared between them Hank threw eventually, and to be honest, quite fucking happily too.

The erotic skirmishes tended to end with her riding him like one of Odin's glorious Valkyries. Golden hair billowing about her shoulders, breasts bouncing, skin shimmering with a sheen of sweat their mutual workout evoked, and her heavenly sheath squeezing him like a velvet vise.

Oh yeah.

He made a mental note to always allow his kitten to have the upper hand when they wrestled. Thoughts of her mounting him in all her beauty, had his cock growing hard again. The long steel appendage bumped against her thighs, and he hissed at the brush of heated skin against his own.

Amber-eyes opened slowly, and Annabeth gifted him with the sweetest smile he'd ever seen. Fuck, what he wouldn't give to see that expression on her face every single morning for the rest of his life.

Hank bent his head, dropping a soft kiss on her mouth just as his sensitized ears picked up the push-cart, stopping outside the door. A brief knock, then the server walked away.

"Good morning," she whispered shyly against his lips.

Hank pressed his kiss deeper, loving the way she responded so readily to him. Eyes locked on hers, he moved between the heaven of her creamy thighs. Her wet nether lips kissed his mushroomed head, and he held himself there, just this side of heaven, and held her stare as he slid inch by inch into her warm, slick heat.

The cushion of her feminine curves was so soft, so warm, so deliciously welcoming. He'd never felt as if he belonged anywhere, but right there, in Annabeth's arms and inside her heavenly sex. He knew of no other place in existence that felt so right.

She was his home. His reason. His heart.

Mate. Love. Mine.

Hank kissed her again. His tongue slid deep into her mouth, lips caressing, eyes open, he watched her reactions closely. So intimate. So precious. He made love to the sweet she-Cat as if the hounds of Hell were on his tail, and with a desperation he'd never experienced.

Not rushed though. No, never that. In fact, quite the opposite. So slowly, ever-so-thoroughly, Hank tried to show her without words what he was feeling. No good with emotions, or with vocalizing them, he loved Annabeth with his body.

Trying to demonstrate with every kiss, nibble, stroke, and caress just what the past few days had meant to him. Leisurely, meticulously, he burrowed into her body the way she had in his heart.

Holding her to him tenderly as he stroked her inside and out, from top to bottom, he trembled with need. Hungry for her, only her. His Falcon cried out with love, hoping to move her to mate him with his song. Silly creature did not realize she could not hear him. But Hank heard him. And he felt her everywhere. It was, in a word, profound.

Annabeth's orgasm was his triumph. It began just as softly as their lovemaking had. The fluttering of her lips around his shaft was tempered by his long, deep strokes. It was a constant squeeze, a steady flex, a slow burn that touched him, enveloped him from head to toe, and everywhere in between.

"Annabeth, my Annabeth," he whispered into her mouth.

Her name was an entreaty on his lips. A petition. His salvation.

Please, he begged, *please.*

Pleasure rose from deep within. It built higher and higher until it became immeasurable. The small, swerving pulsations kept her body taut and on the brink. Then he switched directions, rubbing his pubis into her mound, keeping his thrusts shallow, filling her with him, only him, all of him, until he found the right spot.

Annabeth moaned, a throaty growl of a purring sound. His Gyrfalcon screeched. Then, together, they reached the pinnacle. Warmth coated his cock as she fisted him with her sheath, milking his cum and touching heaven together. As they were meant to.

Mine, growled his raptor.

Yes, echoed Hank.

She was his. And he was ready to do something about it. He smiled and kissed her flushed face as he withdrew from her flesh. Neither could contain their groans at the loss of the other.

Fuck, but he felt empty without her.

Adrift without the anchor that was her sweet core. He was being silly. They had to eat, after all, and he would finish telling her with words this time that this was real. Just as soon as he fed her.

"Be right back, love," Hank whispered and dropped a kiss on her lips.,

Having her there in his bed, cheeks flushed, eyes glittering, was about the best damn thing he'd ever seen, he thought with a satisfied grin. Hank retreated to grab a pair of boxers before claiming the cart from the hallway.

His head was filled with dizzying daydreams, and the million ways he was going to tell Annabeth he loved her and wanted her for keeps. Maybe that was why he hadn't heard what was going on inside the room. When he returned, the bed was empty. Confused, he looked around and waited a beat. Annabeth must have gone to the bathroom.

Frowning, he tried for patience—waited an entire minute, or maybe less. Then he was on his feet, knocking on the bathroom door.

"Annabeth?" he called out then tried again. "Annabeth?"

No answer. Craning his head, he listened for sounds beyond the running water, but there were none. Weird. Another ten seconds ticked by, then panic began to set in.

Before he could talk himself out of it, Hank used his supernatural strength and pushed the door in, splintering the wooden frame.

One look about the plain beige-tiled cubicle, and he knew she was gone. The bathroom window was open.

Clue.

Screeched his Gyrfalcon inside his overtired brain. He registered two things. The curtain had been carelessly torn aside, and the screen had been kicked clean through.

Fuck.

There was no other scent. It was Annabeth who'd done the damage. She'd left him, and he could hardly stand the thought. He slammed a fist through the wall as fury and despair punched a hole right through his gut.

Opening his mouth, Hank threw his head back and released the heartbroken cry of his Gyrfalcon.

She's gone. Really gone.

His sweet, perfect Annabeth had run away. She left him. Alone, so utterly alone.

Fuck. Fuck. FUCK!

It was not her fault. He was to blame. Annabeth had just believed him when he said he didn't want her. How many fucking times had he said it?

Fucking prick.

He'd told her often enough how he was expected to honor his promise to his parents. But how could he do that now? Now that he'd met her, how could he possibly think of anyone else?

Maybe he was a shit. Maybe he was unworthy of her. But she was his mate. His fated mate.

Mate. Mine.

His Falcon cried again, the sound deafening, but still nothing compared to the roaring fury of his heart. The next thing he did, after his momentary panic, was to rip off his boxers.

He might still be able to catch his runaway mate if he hauled ass. Sprinting to the window, he morphed into his Gyrfalcon and took off to the skies.

Sure, people used the term eagle eyes to refer to someone with excellent vision, but falcons had quite the superior eyesight as well. Able to process flashes of light at a much higher frequency than humans or other Shifters, birds of prey had the best damned peepers around when it came to hunting.

A flash of gold had him turning towards the woods that edged up to the far side of the parking lot of the hotel. With a mighty screech, he flapped his wings and circled left, hunting for his errant mate.

But she was too good a huntress. Her evasive

maneuvers were expert, and after circling for hours, he gave up. Finally, Hank returned to the suite. Perhaps she was still there. But she wasn't. In fact, the room had been emptied. Every piece of luggage was gone.

Fucking hell.

There was no way he was going to just sit around. But what could he do? He tried calling the front desk and asking after her, but they refused to give him any information. Then he tried reaching the organizers of the event, only to be told their guest list was confidential.

Hank tossed his phone across the bed, which was, of course, when it rang, and he dove for it.

"Annabeth?"

"Hello there, Hank. Sorry to disappoint you," his Uncle Uzzi said, and he could practically see the old man's smirk.

Fuck.

He'd eat crow with a shovel if the man would just tell him where his mate was. Pain and panic made his stomach clench and his heart stutter in his chest. What if he'd lost her for good?

No, please no.

He needed her back. Hank would do anything at all just to have the chance to tell her how much he loved her. She could have anything, everything, if she would just listen.

Mate. Mine.

The words felt good, even if he was only thinking it. She was his fated mate, and he was a total dick for not claiming her the second he first saw her.

"Uncle Uzzi, I messed up," he said.

"Don't I know it," the Witch growled at him, and he ducked his head like he had when he was just a fledgling.

"You should know better than to spit in the face of destiny, Hank. I certainly taught you better than that," Uncle Uzzi snarled at him in his anger, but Hank took it like man. He deserved that and more.

"I know, Uncle Uzzi. I am so sorry. What do I do?"

"Tell me why you want to do anything first, nephew of mine?" he asked.

"Because Uncle Uzzi, you were right," he said and swallowed hard, running a hand over his face.

"Annabeth is my fated mate."

"I see. And is that all?"

He flinched at the question. Was that all? What else was there? But even as he thought it, he knew the answer.

"No, that is not all. Annabeth is everything. She is

my whole life. I love her, Uncle Uzzi, please help me."

A knock had him rushing to the door, and there he stood, Uncle Uzzi, in the flesh. Wearing a white suit with a pale blue shirt that complimented his sapphire eyes.

The man had come to his rescue, he hoped. But judging from the way the Witch glared at him, he couldn't be sure.

"So, lost your pussy, have you?"

"Uh—"

"Hank, I don't know if you deserve my help, but I believe you when you say you love her. So here I am," he said and pushed inside the room, and for the first time in hours, Hank exhaled.

"I will do anything you say, Uncle Uzzi."

"Maybe you aren't a birdbrain after all," the old Witch remarked and smirked. "Let's get to work."

Hank nodded his assent. He might have started this whole thing ass-backwards, but he wasn't usually slow-witted.

Uncle Uzzi had the best reputation in the business, but beyond that, he loved the old man as he would have loved his own parents if they let him. He'd been a fool not to listen to him.

Sure, he would have to grovel. But it was worth it. Annabeth was so worth it.

"Anything you say, Uncle Uzzi. I promise, I will do it."

"Good," he said and turned, and his fingers alit with dancing blue magic sparks as a smile spread across his weathered face.

"Now, are you ready to pay attention? I will not have you toying with her emotions again, Hank. If you are not sure about Annabeth, I have other suitors who might prove a better match for the Lioness—"

"Mine," he snarled, and Uncle Uzzi's smile grew wider.

"Excellent!"

Chapter Eleven

"How could having hot, mind-blowing, coochie-breaking sex be a bad thing, *AB?*" Toni asked, using her nickname for Annabeth, while daintily chewing on a mouthful of cookie dough.

After Annabeth had hightailed it out of her hotel suite, she'd snagged some towels from the pool area and went back inside to inquire who EWLP had sent to the convention in her stead.

Lucky for her, it was her sister.

She'd known instinctively that Hank was still outside, having taken to the skies in his feathered form when she'd made it back to the lobby. Taking the chance, she had the hotel clerk give her a key to her sister's suite, but first she went back and grabbed her things from her old room.

The delicious scent of Hank and the naughty, *very naughty,* things he'd done to her perfumed the air, and she'd been hard pressed to leave. But she could not stay there and accept the crumbs he offered. Not when she loved him like she did.

Stupid clingy kitty.

Forcing her feet to work, one in front of the other, Annabeth made it to her sister's room. Once there, she'd collapsed on one of the beds, gut-wrenching sobs wracking her towel-clad frame, until Toni pulled out the big guns. Or in this case, the big menu.

Ice cream by the bucket, cookie dough, the edible kind guaranteed to not hurt her sometimes sensitive belly, and a bottle of tequila to boot. Once her sweet tooth had been sated, and she tossed back her tenth shot, Annabeth finally confessed everything that had happened between her and Hank.

"Because, Toni—*I love him,* and he was just servicing me. Like I'm a fucking car or something," she wailed and buried her head in the pillow.

"Yeah, but Hank loves cars. He's like *cliterally* a limo driver," she said and grinned. "Like that? I just made that up."

"OMG! Shut up, Toni. And really, maybe it was a heat thing, but I swear, I have never had sex feel like that before. He was just so, so," she said and shook her head as words failed to describe what they'd shared.

Her Falcon lover had played her body like Elton John played a piano. He was, in a word, sublime, tending to every one of her hidden fantasies and desires. Every naughtily whispered direction, every erotic dream was fulfilled effortlessly. He'd made her wishes come true before she even knew what they were.

That last coming together had literally torn her heart from her chest. The heat cycle was over, but Hank had slid into her so sweetly, she couldn't refuse. It was like he'd become her own personal blanket, covering her with his large, muscular body. He'd filled her so deep, loved her so good, and when she came. Fuck. It was fantastic. On and on, her endless orgasm had spanned centuries, countless miles, until all she could think, see, breathe, hear, taste, and feel was him.

Hank.

Mine.

Mate.

Only, he was not her mate. Sure, she'd sensed the

time or three when he wanted to mark her during her explosive heat, but she would not allow it. How could she, under those circumstances?

No. He would hate or resent her in the end. Wasn't that why her own father had left? After delivering four girls, her father had tried to stick it out. He'd mated her mother, who, following a fifth heat, finally gave birth to a son, but in the end, Patricia Golden had wound up alone.

Her mother was not one to mince words. She'd told her children quite candidly what had occurred between their parents. Never spoke ill of the deadbeat either, despite Annabeth's resolve to maim the fucker if she ever saw him. But what it had taught the Lioness was priceless.

Love could not be forced.

If it wasn't there, it just wasn't, and there was nothing anyone could do about it. She might love Hank Garret, but the Gyrfalcon Shifter did not love her. That was as glaring a truth as any.

"Well, I mean, going into your heat couldn't have been that bad?" Toni hedged.

Annabeth supposed she should have considered the fact that all of her siblings would experience the same sooner rather than later. Trying to smile, she faced Antonette. The female was absolutely beautiful. Had even modeled for an X-rated magazine if the rumors were true.

"I'm sorry," Annabeth said. "Did I mention? Best. Sex. Ever."

"Yeah," Toni said and blushed. "You kinda did. But AB, what if you're pregnant?"

Her breathing stopped at the thought. Hope filled her and crushed her heart at the same time. She would be so happy to have Hank's young.

"Oh," she said, eyes wide. "I will do what Mom did. I will raise my cubs with all the love I have in my heart, and besides, they will have the best aunts and uncle ever, right?" she asked with a watery smile.

"They sure as fuck will," Toni said and grabbed her in a fierce hug.

"I just didn't expect to love him, I guess."

Foolish, foolish girl.

"Oh AB, the heart wants what it wants, and all that jazz," Toni replied, sniffed, then flippantly bounced off the bed and hurled a shopping bag at Annabeth, "Come on, get dressed."

"Dressed? What for?"

"The con ends tonight."

"With the ball? Fuck, Toni, I don't want to go."

"Too bad," her sister snapped. "You know, I did all this for you. Took over and all, the least you can do is come with me tonight. Besides, it's not just the dance. First, the *New Jersey Convention for Quality Food Products*, which, as you know, is secretly Shifter run, is giving an award to their newest members. Second, I hear Mason Lane sent a new batch of his latest whiskey flavor, *Rose Bite,* to the con."

"Oh, yeah?" Annabeth feigned interest as she stood up and opened the bag.

Toni loved to shop. She was a clotheshorse, and everything looked great on her. But her sister also had a natural eye for what looked good on others. Without thinking too much about it, Annabeth resigned herself to getting dressed and listening to Toni ramble on about whiskey and shoes—her only true passions. It was the least she could do.

"Well?" Annabeth asked a while later and twirled in front of her sister.

Toni was resplendent in a red strapless dress that highlighted her long, sleek legs, and killer figure. Annabeth would probably hate her if she didn't love her so much.

Rawr.

"That looks gorgeous on you," Toni said and grinned like the cat that got the canary, reaching out to snag the tag Annabeth had accidentally left on.

The dress was a dream with fluttery sleeves, a

cinched waist, plunging neckline, and a skirt that flared out gracefully, ending just above her knees. It was perfect, except for the color.

The jewel tone made her want to cry. It was the same cobalt blue that reminded her painfully of Hank's brilliant, piercing gaze.

"You ready?"

"As I'll ever be, sis," Annabeth replied, smile trembling as she forced herself to go numb.

Normally, she loved going out with one or all of her siblings. Lionesses loved to party. But not tonight. Annabeth's emotions had been through the wringer the past few days. She wanted to curl up in fetal position and stay there for a day, or a month, or a year—*just until the ache in her heart went away.*

"Isn't this place beautiful?" Toni asked, spinning around like a supermodel on the runway.

Heads turned and growls sounded, but Toni was oblivious as she took in the decorations of the hotel's beautiful ballroom. Annabeth giggled as a few males close enough to witness Antonette's graceful spin developed an immediate case of broken-neck syndrome.

Idiots.

"Yeah, it's nice," Annabeth said and shook her head at Toni's *what* expression.

"Oh, look," she pointed to the dais where one of the convention representatives was speaking.

"What?"

"They are inducting the new members now."

Annabeth followed her sister to the edge of the crowd to listen to the speaker. Her heart wasn't in it. But she supposed it was better than crying over spilled milk. Her heart being the milk in this scenario.

Ugh. That metaphor sucked.

Whatever, I'm mourning the loss of my love. Gimme a break, kitty!

Rawr.

Annabeth rolled her eyes at her inner Lioness. Her Cat was pissed at her, and really, she could not blame the creature. Annabeth had fucked this whole thing up. But, she was paying for it. Boy, was she ever.

"Good evening, everyone. We have a special announcement, folks. After some debate, *and a sizeable donation,* we are adding a *Guest Services and Hospitality* section to our convention this year," he said, and a smattering of applause broke out among those gathered.

Annabeth accepted the glass of champagne from a passing server. She feigned interest, tried to walk away, but Toni pulled her back. Apparently, her sis was invested in this whatever the hell it was.

Whatever.

"As a thank you to our new partners, we offer this award on behalf of the *New Jersey Convention for Quality Food Products* to the owner of *Falcon Limousine Services,* Hank Garret."

The announcer handed a small plaque to the familiar tall, handsome man dressed in an impeccable black tuxedo, who stood beside him on the dais. Thunder roared in her ears as Annabeth took in his wide shoulders encased in ultra-fine black fabric.

It can't be him.

Her heart pounded and her inner kitty roared, desperate to get close to the man who'd owned her, body heart and soul for the past two days.

He should be gone. On his way to the North American Tower meeting. The tailored jacket outlined his musculature to the point where Annabeth noted several interested eyes and whispers. She almost lost her shit. Wanted to bare her fangs and eat those bitches just for ogling her man.

Eeep!

Hank was not hers. She better remember that. But what was he doing here?

"Easy, kitty," a familiar voice said, and she turned to see Uncle Uzzi smiling as Hank accepted the plaque and said a few words on behalf of the company.

"Hank is the owner of Falcon Limousine Services?" Toni asked, having joined them.

Her sister loosed a wolf whistle that made Annabeth's Lioness rise angrily. Which, of course, only made Antonette smile wider. The heifer.

"I see. It's like that, huh, sis?"

Toni laughed, cutting off the sound, as she watched Hank shake hands with the reps.

"So that's him, huh? Want me to gut him? I have a tarp in the truck that will do nicely. We won't even mess up the hotel room."

Oh, how quickly her sister's admiration of Hank's assets turned bloodthirsty! Loyalty and sisterly love were two of Annabeth's favorite things. She whimpered and nodded at her sister.

"Yes, that is him," she said.

"Yes, but you might refrain a moment on the maiming, my dears," Uncle Uzzi offered. He winked at Annabeth's sister, then looked at her.

"Hank is my nephew, after all, and I prefer him in one piece. Even if he is a birdbrain sometimes."

"The callous jerk hurt my sister. I think he deserves a good thrashing. AB? What do you say?"

"No!"

Annabeth shook her head, oblivious to the identical grins on their faces.

"I don't want him hurt, Toni. I love him. Even if he is a jerk. You were right, Uncle Uzzi. You found my mate. But it was not meant to be," she whispered her explanation, tears building in her eyes. "It's not anyone's fault. Look, no one, not even you, Uncle, Uzzi, could have guessed he wouldn't want me back—"

"You're wrong," a deep voice sounded from behind her, cutting her off, and Annabeth went still.

"He does want you back. More than he wants to breathe. I'm so sorry, Annabeth."

She turned around rapidly, dropping the glass of champagne in her hand. Hank lunged and caught it before it could shatter, handing it off to Uncle Uzzi or Toni, she was not sure which. Her eyes were on his face, and what she saw there stunned her.

"Annabeth, please, I am so sorry for acting like a complete asshole. Please let me explain," he began.

"You shouldn't be here, Hank."

"Where should I be?"

"I don't know. On your way to the North American Tower I assume, to find your mate," she growled between gritted teeth, turning her back on him despite her Lioness' furious snarl that she remain to hear him out.

No. He doesn't deserve us.

He is our mate. Stay. Listen.

"Give me another chance, please. I don't deserve it, but I am begging you, Annabeth. Hear me out," he said, his voice laced with a soul-deep desperation that tugged on all her heartstrings.

He reached out and grabbed her arm gently with one enormous hand.

Dammit.

He was the only man she knew who could make her feel small and cherished, protected, even, by his sheer bulk alone.

"Fine," she said, ignoring Toni, who was standing behind him making throat-slicing gestures.

"Not here," he said, one perfectly arched eyebrow rising as he took in her sister's antics.

"Uh, will you come outside to speak to me? Please."

"Toni," she hissed at her sister, who wore an expression of feigned innocence when called out.

Annabeth exhaled and closed her eyes briefly. She wanted to go with him. Every instinct she had said to go listen to the man. She just wasn't sure if she could trust herself around him.

The crisp, cool scent of spring breezes washed over her, and she felt warmth seep from his body through the suddenly too-tight dress she wore. Hell, her heat might be over, but she wanted him with a ferocity she'd never believed herself capable of. Her breasts swelled, and sex grew slick with desire as he guided her through the crowd by the elbow. She noted the flare of his nostrils, and the rumble in his chest.

Shit, he'd picked up on her arousal.

It was not something she could hide from him, stupid Falcon smelling senses. Her awareness of his enhanced olfactory abilities did nothing to hide her embarrassment.

She paused briefly in the lobby, looking for a chair, but Hank must have already had a destination in mind. He led her outside, to where his Rolls Royce sat waiting for them.

"After you," he said and opened the door for her.

He held her hand while she scooched inside. Annabeth slid across the smooth, cool leather of the seats. The limo had recently been cleaned and vacuumed. There was a bouquet of pink roses on the seat opposite them, a box of expensive chocolates, and champagne on ice.

Someone sure was intent on making a good impression. But Annabeth felt too raw and bruised to be moved by such trinkets. Her stomach tensed, and it was difficult to breathe. Once so full of hope, but now her bruised heart was too afraid to believe.

Trusting—that's what she'd been when she had run into Uncle Uzzi of the famous Uncle Uzzi's Magical Matchmaking Service. Trusting, naïve, and plan old gullible.

"I thought it was kismet," she whispered.

"What?"

"Oh, nothing," she replied and shook her head.

Annabeth swallowed, inching closer to the other side of the seat, flinching when he moved his big body in next to her. She noted his gasp and hated that she'd hurt him. But what did he expect?

"Oh, Annabeth, I am so sorry. I don't blame you for being wary of my motives," he began with a shaky breath.

His big, luminous eyes met hers, and she sucked in a breath. There was so much feeling in those beautiful blue pools she could drown in them.

"What is this about, Hank? You don't have to worry about anything. If my heat was successful, I will raise the cubs and let you know when they are born, but you don't have to—"

"Cubs? Oh, shit," he hissed, and she realized he had never even considered the possibility.

Closing her eyes on how stupid she'd been, Annabeth tried for calm, but failed. Tears leaked down her face, ruining her makeup, but she didn't care as she reached for the handle.

"Stop, please, baby. Don't cry." Hank took her hand and pulled her back so that his chest was pressed against hers, his lips nuzzling her neck.

"I just never thought—"

"Well, what did you expect? It's why we have a heat cycle," she said, allowing herself to indulge in his embrace for a single moment before she struggled against him.

"Let me go, Hank."

He shook his head, his arms wrapped around her like steel bands.

"I can't." he whispered, holding her tighter. "Stop, please, Annabeth. I don't want you to go—"

"Why? Because I might be pregnant?" Annabeth sobbed, the hurt only spreading now with his insufferable integrity.

"No. Yes. Yes and no," he said, hissing when her

elbow caught him in the gut, but he still refused to loosen his hold on her.

Annabeth stopped struggling. She fought for air, then decided to try to reason with him. Hard to do when all his deliciousness was pressed so intimately against her. The arms that had held her captive were softer now, gentler, hands stroking her sides, her back, the swells of her breasts.

"Please stop, Hank. I won't run, but I need to talk to you face to face and I can't think with you touching me," she confessed. Might as well tell him everything.

Dangerous, sexy man held her heart in his talons. He could crush her at will. Never had another person held such power over Annabeth, but Hank Garret held it all. His hold tightened briefly before he did as she asked, letting her go so she could meet that glowing cobalt stare of his.

"I knew from the first moment I saw you, you were mine. My fated mate," she said, stopping him with a raised hand when he moved as if to touch her again.

"But it wasn't like that for you. You never wanted me. Not as a mate. Not as anything. Uncle Uzzi might have introduced us, but it was my heat that tempted you to my bed."

"That's not true—"

"That is true, and it is okay. You're not to blame here. You serviced a female Shifter in her heat, and now you feel responsible, but I am telling you it is unnecessary. You can still go to the Tower. Find your real mate. I will be fine, Hank. I am a survivor. All the Goldens are," she said and tried to smile, but it felt wrong and she couldn't see because her eyes were full of tears.

Fucking hell. This hurt. It was tearing her apart, but it needed to be done. Hank was good and had a ridiculous sense of honor. She had to let him go. It was the only way.

"You're right. You will be fine no matter what, Annabeth because you are the most extraordinary woman I have ever met, but you forgot something," he said.

"What?"

"ME! You forgot me! I won't be fine, dammit. Not without you," he cried out, voice hoarse with emotion.

"Hank?" she whispered, tears flowing, Annabeth covered her mouth with her hand and watched disbelieving as he cupped her face and bore his heart to her. Moisture dripped from his eyes, but he wouldn't let go or look away, he just held her, and told her everything.

"I need you. I won't make it. Not unless you are with me. You, Annabeth, it's always been *you*." Hank dropped his head to her forehead for one second before pulling back, making sure she could see the truth in his eyes as he finished it.

"I know I don't deserve a second chance. I've been stupid and stubborn. But I swear to the gods I will spend the rest of my life making it up to you if you give me another chance."

"How can I trust you?" she asked in a small voice she hardly recognized.

"Because I love you, Annabeth," he said simply.

Annabeth shook her head. It was too much. She couldn't take it.

"I'm sorry," she said, and turned to leave.

But Hank was stubborn. She should have remembered that as she pulled away from him and exited his car. The sound of a Falcon screeching filled her ears, and Annabeth's Lioness wanted to roar her response, but she locked the beast down.

Pulling off her heels, she ran back to the ballroom. Her heart somewhere on the floor as she joined Toni at the bar.

"Sis?"

"I need to leave," Annabeth whispered.

"Okay," Toni said and grabbed her hand, but as Annabeth turned, she collided with a familiar shape.

"Baby doll, you left me in the lurch there with that big pigeon of yours. Now, that he's flown the coop, what say you and me, we do a little dancing of our own?" Luca Bianco said and waggled his eyebrows.

Annabeth was so addled she had to stop and think about his words. She hardly realized he put his hands on her, till her inner animal began to spit and hiss.

"You smell good, baby. You know I got plenty cows at home in my barn, but I could always use a little action after a hard day's work."

"Luca, get lost!" Toni snarled over her shoulder, but the Bull still didn't take the hint.

Her sister took Annabeth's hand, but Luca was stronger than she realized. With little effort, he tugged Annabeth out of Toni's grip. The Lioness inside her snarled, but before she could react, Hank was there.

He knocked the Bull on the shoulder with an open palm causing the huge man to turn to face him. Oooh and the man was pissed. Power radiated from Hank in waves. Dominance, the likes of which rivaled that of the King of the Blue Valley Pride himself, pulsed from him, making it hard for even Annabeth to breathe.

Hank wasn't just a Gyrfalcon and the owner of *Falcon Limousine Service*. He was a motherfucking Alpha.

"Thought I told you, hands off," Hank snarled, and then the typically staid Falcon did something Annabeth never would have expected.

He started a bar brawl. His very first, she was sure. And all because of her.

Sexy possessive man. My man.

How lucky could one girl be? Annabeth practically swooned as the Bull Shifter went ass over teakettle when her mate punched him right in the face. Of course, the idiot flayed his arms like a schoolgirl and spilled his drink all over Annabeth's new dress.

That in turn caused some beyotch from *Chicken Little's Chicken Farms* to cackle uncontrollably at Annabeth's soaked state. Which made Toni jump on the redhead, smacking the woman's face with the peanut basket that had been sitting on the bar.

"Are you okay?" Hank asked, rushing to her side.

"I am, but I think you started a little something here," she said and grinned as the attendees of the

New Jersey Convention for Quality Food Products erupted into a full-blown barroom fight.

Even the band was in on it. The few members left standing started playing a terrible cover of Elton John's *Saturday Nights Alright for Fighting*. Annabeth giggled and Hank looked around wide-eyed as bodies and drinks and a whole charcuterie board went flying past them.

"Shit. Come on," he said, pulling her behind an upturned table for some cover.

"Hank, what was that about?" she asked.

"I guess my Falcon didn't like his hands on you," Hank said, all seriousness.

"Why?"

Annabeth knew it was dangerous, but she felt like pushing him just a little bit farther. She needed to know. There was no way she had the strength to run a second time.

"Because, kitten, you're mine."

"Am I?"

"Oh, yeah. All mine," he said and grinned against her lips.

Hank kissed her for minutes or hours, she couldn't tell, lost as she was in his arms.

"Annabeth," he breathed her name, pressing his

forehead to hers with one hand cupped firmly behind her neck and the other on her waist.

"Yeah?"

"I love you. You are my mate, and I want to claim you. I believe we are fated, my sweet Lioness. If you will have me?" he asked, and she knew he was sincere.

"Yes," she replied, ducking when a pitcher went flying overhead.

"Watch out!"

"Come here," she said, and tugged him into a crawl. He followed her behind the bar, and when she pushed him against the wall, it was with the intention of kissing him with all the feeling she'd been keeping locked up and buried.

This time, there was no heat to hide behind. This time, their passion was just for each other. It was all Annabeth and Hank. The two of them committing to each other in front of the gods and Fates combined.

But before their lips could meet and Annabeth and Hank could consummate their feelings, a familiar voice interrupted.

"Hello my dears! Now, I am happy to see you have made up, but I think you two should go claim each other somewhere a little safer," Uncle Uzzi said and winked from his own position, crouched behind the bar sharing a bottle of tequila with Toni.

"Uncle Uzzi? Toni? What about you?"

"Don't you worry about us," Toni winked, claws bared.

"It's been a long time since I've been involved in a Shifter showdown."

"Yes, and I have magic on our side. Now you two skedaddle, but I want pictures when those cubs are born."

"Yes, Uncle Uzzi," Annabeth replied, kissing the older man's cheek.

"Thank you so much, Uncle Uzzi," Hank said, following suit.

"No worries. Now get going before this gets too rough for your female," Uncle Uzzi instructed.

He waved his hand and blue sparks shot into the air and caught a couple of bottles of booze that someone had lobbed at their heads.

"Will you two be okay?" Hank asked again.

"Hank, I will kick your ass if you ask me that again. Now shoo!" Toni yelled.

Annabeth grinned up at Hank, who was gazing down into her eyes like the sun rose and set on her.

"Hank?"

"Yeah?"

"Take me home. Make me yours."

Mate. Finally.

She sighed as he tugged her to him. Lifting her in his arms, he sped out the door unscathed.

Rawr!

Epilogue

T hank fuck Hank had kept the hotel room, which was a good idea in hindsight. No way would he have been able to bear driving back to Blue Valley or Manhattan—where they both lived.

The decision on where they would build their lives would have to wait. Truth was, he didn't care, as long as he had Annabeth beside him.

Hank slammed the door to their room closed. Mouth locked on hers, he tore at her soaked dress, cursing the asshole who'd spilled his drink on her.

Should go back. Punch that fucker again, his bird growled.

As if she sensed his turn of thought, Annabeth reached between them, cupping his dick in her firm hands, and everything else slipped away into the periphery of his mind. There was only one person who existed at the forefront of his thoughts. And she was everything.

Her. His mate.

The one and only female he would ever take as his own.

"Are you sure, Hank," she said, slowing down for a moment to look up at him.

Her golden eyes glowed softly in the dimly lit room. The air around her shimmered and swayed with the softly pulsing illumination that seemed to come from her warm ivory skin and honey-colored hair.

"Annabeth, I was sure two seconds into meeting you," he confessed, aware of the slight widening of her eyes and flare of her nostrils.

"Really?"

"Yes, really. I am so sorry I wasted so much time. I thought I had to keep the promise I made to my father, but I did not make that promise for any of the right reasons. I was looking for approval from a man who did not approve of anything about me" he confessed.

"I am so sorry, Hank."

"Don't be. You taught me what real love is, Annabeth. It's accepting someone for who they are, not what. It's smiles given freely. It's having faith and trusting someone with your heart. I promised my father I would carry on our line, and I mean to keep that promise."

Annabeth gasped, but Hank powered on, making sure she understood him.

"I will honor my vow by carrying on my line with you. *With you, Annabeth.* You are my mate. You are everything I have ever wanted. Love you," he whispered, touching her face reverently.

"Oh, Hank. It's alright. Everything is okay," she replied. "I understand you were going through something, and I am so glad you found your way back to me. I love you, Hank. We have forever. Starting right now."

"How did I get so lucky? I don't deserve you."

"Yes, you do."

"Thank you, Annabeth. You give me everything," he growled, overcome with emotion for this sweet, precious woman.

My woman.

Hank took a moment to gaze at his mate's luscious, bountiful curves. She was a work of art. Perfection personified, and she was his. Finally.

"I look at you, and I lose all sense of space and

time. You're a treasure, kitten. I love you completely. Let me show you," he whispered, then claimed her mouth.

He was impatient, but so was she. Licking his way down her body, Hank buried his face between her creamy thighs, spreading her wide. She yelled his name, and it was music to his ears as he feasted on her. Annabeth screamed again and fisted his hair, rolling her hips and grinding her sex against the flat of his tongue.

"Yes, more," she yelled.

He did his best to comply. His lusty little Lioness was so damned sexy, he almost came from listening to her whimpers and cries. The second he felt her pussy ripple around him, he was on her.

Sliding up her body, Hank gripped the base of his cock, aligning his head with her slit, then he pushed in. Stretching her walls, Annabeth clung to his shoulders, moaning at his invasion.

She was so slick and hot, her sex still trembling with the aftermath of her first orgasm. First of many, he promised as he drove into her welcoming flesh. In and out, he made love to his sweet mate, grunting as her claw-tipped fingers pierced the skin on his hips.

"Fuck, baby, you're so tight," he growled and moved sharply, swallowing her cries of pleasure.

"Claim me, Hank," she commanded, and he was more than ready to do the job.

He lowered his head, sucking on that piece of flesh he'd been eying between her shoulder and her neck. Flexing his hips, he buried himself deep, stroking her tight walls and rubbing her clit with every swivel and swirl of his hips. Annabeth locked her legs around him, scratching his hips.

Then he struck. Biting down, he held her in place, moving harder, faster, and deeper while wave after wave of orgasmic bliss filled her. His own climax rushing through as she pierced the skin of his chest above his heart with her own fangs.

"Mine," she growled, in a throaty feline purr that had his cock ready to burst again.

"Guess I had it right the first time," he said, a wicked grin spread across his face as he looked down into her twin golden pools, "I'm yours."

"Yeah?" Annabeth smiled, and it was like the sun shining on him. She nuzzled him with her nose and lips, dropping loud kisses on his flesh, marking him in every way that counted.

"Fuck. Yeah. This Falcon's heart belongs to you, kitten."

"Guess that makes *me* the cat who got the canary."

"Annabeth, I love you. But that is truly an awful pun," he growled.

Annabeth laughed. Snorted. Then laughed some more. And wasn't that fucking adorable?

Hank sighed, then moaned, as he tickled her into submission. Their playful antics quickly turned erotic, and he proclaimed his love loudly, filling her once more with his hardened length.

"I love you, Annabeth. You are the only woman I ever want to mate. Forever," he growled.

"Mine," she echoed.

"Yessssss."

Kak kak kak kak!

Rawwwwwrrrr!

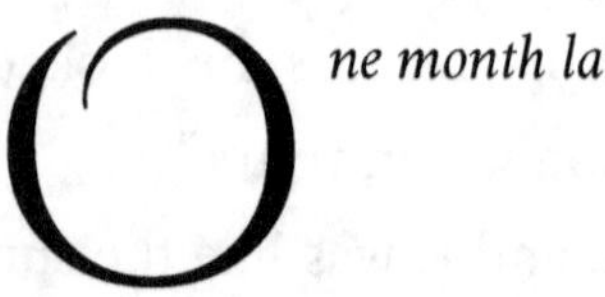

One *ne month later...*

. . .

Hank and Annabeth entered her old apartment in Blue Valley Pride, where they were moving in until they settled on a nice house to build their dream family. Sighing happily, Hank carried her over the threshold kissing her silly for a moment before letting her stand on her own.

"Hey, love," he whispered, smiling so bright it almost hurt to not look at him.

"Mmm. Hang on," Annabeth said, realizing she needed to do some recon first.

She had truly lucked out with a mate who was happy to be wherever she wanted, and that included being near her job and Pride. Despite the antics her family, the Goldens, sometimes got into.

"Honey, just wait for me in the living room."

"Why?"

But she just raised one finger and bit her lip before pushing the door open to their bedroom.

"I just need to check the bedroom really quickly," Annabeth said, running back to kiss her mate hard on the lips one more time.

"Want help?"

"No, I got it," she said before running off to see if

her prankster siblings had done anything untoward to welcome her mate into the fold.

The bed was clear. Thank the gods. The closet too. Now for the bathroom. Eyes narrowed, she opened the door, exhaling when it was just as plain and clean as ever.

Happy rawr.

Annabeth was relieved her family had taken her messages to heart when she'd told them her mate was not used to their kind of boisterous activities. He'd mated her, but she was hoping for marriage as well. And there was no way he would agree to that if they scared the poor guy to death.

"Hey, love?"

"Yeah?" she replied, ears straining to hear anything that might hint what he was trying so hard to conceal.

"I think someone sent us a little gift basket," Hank growled, and Annabeth came rushing to the living room to find her tall, gorgeous mate holding an enormous gilt birdcage filled with an assortment of X-rated bird-themed goodies.

OHMYFUCKINGGAWD. I am gonna kill them.

Annabeth approached warily. Hank's eyes glowed blue with his Falcon. His jaw clenched. And his nostrils flared. He cocked his head to the side, perusing the gift basket.

"Do you suppose they meant the feathered strap on for you or me?" Hank asked with one eyebrow raised.

"Uh, I am assuming me," she replied and blushed furiously as he pulled item after item from the basket.

"Let's see what else we have here. Ah, we have edible undies—strawberry flavor. Nice. Birdseed? Oh, ah, and a gallon tub of sunflower seed butter with instructions to *butter up your coochie so the seagull gets to munching*," Hank read off the attached notecard and Annabeth wanted to die.

"Please stop."

"Not done yet, kitten. We have more lube, an assortment of merkins, one fur and all the rest are feathered, and my personal favorite a two-toned bird lure complete with a package of freeze-dried rats."

Hank was biting the inside of his lip, and she did not know if he was going to explode or start laughing. She really hoped the latter.

Sigh.

"Lover, I can explain. It's just my family is a bit

more intense when it comes to the whole practical joking thing," she tried to explain.

But it did not matter. Her mate was already pulling her towards him. His deep chuckle vibrated through her as he locked her in a tight hug, dipping her backwards, and Annabeth released a relieved breath.

Then he was nuzzling her neck, her cheek, and finally Hank was kissing her. All explanations and rational thoughts left Annabeth's head.

"I love you," he growled before tossing her over his shoulder and grabbing the container of sunflower seed butter in his free hand.

"And I know just what to do with this!"

Same day, somewhere else.

Uncle Uzzi smiled broadly as the handsome young Lion opened the door to the limousine before he got in.

"Hello, Uncle Uzzi," the young Lion greeted him.

"You're Carter, aren't you?" he asked.

"Yes, sir. Hank told me to treat you better than I would my own parents, so you just tell me where to go and what to do and I am on it," he replied and smiled charmingly.

"I see," Uncle Uzzi said as a familiar, tingling sensation washed through his veins.

"You just listen to me, Carter, and everything will be fine."

This was going to be a piece of cake! The chocolate gooey kind, he thought and made note for Richard to buy some Dutch chocolate.

The handsome Lion Shifter cocked his head and glanced at the Witch in the rearview mirror before speeding away. It seemed the Uncle Uzzi's Magical Matchmaking Service had another client in its sights.

And this pussy better watch out...

*he end.*

Did you enjoy this story? Look for the rest of the

Maverick Pride Tales on my website here: https://
www.cdgorri.com/series/maverick-pride-tales/.

Or
Check out the Dire Wolf Mates today!

Thank you and happy reading!
Del mare alla stella,
C.D. Gorri

Coming Soon Purrfectly Timed!

*Pierce is on the hunt for someone to call his own, but this
kitty throws him for a loop.*

Pierce McDowd is surrounded by mated pairs, but
he can't seem to find someone to call his own. His
concentration is nil, and his boss has had it with his
mistakes. Forced to take a leave of absence to get his
head on straight, Pierce is determined not to waste
this impromptu vacation.

It's time to bring in the big guns. Decision made,
Pierce makes a call to *Uncle Uzzi's Magical
Matchmaking Service.* If anyone can help him find his
mate, Uncle Uzzi can.

Antonetta Golden is no ordinary Lioness. Labelled trouble by men who could not handle her, this kitty is more than meets that eye. Single and not loving it, her career becomes her focus.

But when Uncle Uzzi calls her with a request, she has a choice to make. She doesn't want to turn the infamous Witch down, but it's her busiest season. Perfect timing just doesn't seem to exist for this Lioness.

Will she learn to compromise to meet the man of her dreams?

Find out if Pierce and Toni get their happy ever after in this installation of the Maverick Pride Tales.

Beware... Here Be Even More Dragons!

The Falk Clan Tales began as my stories surrounding four dragon Brothers and how they find their one true mates, but when a long lost brother arrives on the scene, followed by a few more Shifters…what can I say? The more the merrier!

Each Dragon's chest is marked with his rose, the magical link to his heart and his magic. They each have a matching gemstone to go with it.

She's given up on love. But he's just begun.

In *The Dragon's Valentine* we meet the eldest Falk brother, Callius. He is on a mission to find a Castle and his one true mate, one he can trust with his diamond rose....

His heart is frozen. Can she change his mind about love?

In *The Dragon's Christmas Gift* our attention shifts to Alexsander, the youngest brother of the four. He has resigned himself to a life alone, until he meets *her*.

Some wounds run deep. Can a Dragon's heart be unbroken?

The Dragon's Heart is the story of Edric Falk who has vowed never to love again, but that changes when he meets his feisty mate, Joselyn Curacao.

She just wants a little fun. He's looking for a lifetime.

We finally meet Nikolai Falk and his sexy Shifter mate in *The Dragon's Secret*.

**Now available in a boxed set.*

Guess what…. I've got more Dragons on the way!

Look for The Dragon's Treasure. Now available.

Coming in 2022 The Dragon's Dream and The Dragon's Surprise.

Other Titles by C.D. Gorri

Paranormal Romance Books:

Macconwood Pack Novel Series:

Charley's Christmas Wolf: A Macconwood Pack Novel 1

Cat's Howl: A Macconwood Pack Novel 2

Code Wolf: A Macconwood Pack Novel 3

The Witch and The Werewolf: A Macconwood Pack Novel 4

To Claim a Wolf: A Macconwood Pack Novel 5

Conall's Mate: A Macconwood Pack Novel 6

Her Solstice Wolf: A Macconwood Pack Novel 7

Werewolf Fever: A Macconwood Pack Novel 8

Also available in 2 boxed sets:

The Macconwood Pack Volume 1

The Macconwood Pack Volume 2

Macconwood Pack Tales Series:

Wolf Bride: The Story of Ailis and Eoghan A Macconwood Pack Tale 1

Summer Bite: A Macconwood Pack Tale 2

His Winter Mate: A Macconwood Pack Tale 3

Snow Angel: A Macconwood Pack Tale 4

Charley's Baby Surprise: A Macconwood Pack Tale 5

Home for the Howlidays: A Macconwood Pack Tale 6

A Silver Wedding: A Macconwood Pack Tale 7

Mine Furever: A Macconwood Pack Tale 8

A Furry Little Christmas: A Macconwood Pack Tale 9

Also available in two boxed sets:

The Macconwood Pack Tales Volume 1

Shifters Furever: The Macconwood Pack Tales Volume 2

<u>The Falk Clan Tales:</u>

The Dragon's Valentine: A Falk Clan Novel 1

The Dragon's Christmas Gift: A Falk Clan Novel 2

The Dragon's Heart: A Falk Clan Novel 3

The Dragon's Secret: A Falk Clan Novel 4

The Dragon's Treasure: A Falk Clan Novel 5

The Dragon's Surprise: A Falk Clan Novel 6

The Dragon's Dream: A Falk Clan Novel 7

Dragon Mates: The Falk Clan Series Boxed Set Books 1-4

Dragon Mates 2: The Falk Clan Series Boxed Set Books 5-7

The Bear Claw Tales:

Bearly Breathing: A Bear Claw Tale 1

Bearly There: A Bear Claw Tale 2

Bearly Tamed: A Bear Claw Tale 3

Bearly Mated: A Bear Claw Tale 4

Also available in a boxed set:

The Complete Bear Claw Tales (Books 1-4)

The Barvale Clan Tales:

Polar Opposites: The Barvale Clan Tales 1

Polar Outbreak: The Barvale Clan Tales 2

Polar Compound: A Barvale Clan Tale 3

Polar Curve: A Barvale Clan Tale 4

Also available in a boxed set:

The Barvale Clan Tales (Books 1-4)

Barvale Holiday Tales:

A Bear For Christmas

Hers To Bear

Thank You Beary Much

Bearing Gifts

Also available in a boxed set:

The Barvale Holiday Tales (Books 1-3)

Marked by the Devil: Purely Paranormal Romance Books

Mated to the Dragon King: Purely Paranormal Romance Books

Claimed by the Demon: Purely Paranormal Romance Books

Christmas with a Devil, a Dragon King, & a Demon: Purely Paranormal Romance Books

Vampire Lover: Purely Paranormal Romance Books

Grizzly Lover: Purely Paranormal Romance Books

Christmas With Her Chupacabra: Purely Paranormal Romance Books

Purely Paranormal Romance Books Anthology

The Wardens of Terra:

Bound by Air: The Wardens of Terra Book 1

Star Kissed: A Wardens of Terra Short

Waterlocked: The Wardens of Terra Book 2

Moon Kissed: A Wardens of Terra Short

*Now in a boxed set and in audio!

The Maverick Pride Tales:

Purrfectly Mated

Purrfectly Kissed

Purrfectly Trapped

Purrfectly Caught

Purrfectly Naughty

Purrfectly Bound

Purrfectly Paired

Dire Wolf Mates:

Shake That Sass

Breaking Sass

Pinch of Sass

Kickin' Sass

Wyvern Protection Unit:

Gift Wrapped Protector: WPU 1

Standalones:

The Enforcer

Blood Song: A Sanguinem Council Book

Spring Fling (co-written with P. Mattern)

EveL Worlds:

Chinchilla and the Devil: A FUCN'A Book

Sammi and the Jersey Bull: A FUCN'A Book

Mouse and the Ball: A FUCN'A Book

The Guardians of Chaos:

Wolf Shield: Guardians of Chaos Book1

Dragon Shield: Guardians of Chaos Book 2

Stallion Shield: Guardians of Chaos Book 3

Panther Shield: Guardians of Chaos 4

Witch Shield: Guardians of Chaos 5

Vampire Shield: Guardians of Chaos 6

<u>Howl's Romance</u>

Mated to the Werewolf Next Door: A Howl's Romance

The Tiger King's Christmas Bride

Claiming His Virgin Mate: Howls Romance

<u>Twice Mated Tales</u>

Doubly Claimed

Doubly Bound

Doubly Tied

Twice Mated Tales Anthology

<u>Hearts of Stone Series</u>

Shifter Mountain: Hearts of Stone 1

Shifter City: Hearts of Stone 2

Shifter Village: Hearts of Stone 3

Hearts of Stone Books 1-3 Anthology

<u>Accidentally Undead Series</u>

Fangs For Nothin'

<u>Moongate Island Tales</u>

Moongate Island Mate

Moongate Island Christmas Claim

Mated in Hope Falls

Mated by Moonlight

Speed Dating with the Denizens of the Underworld

Ash: Speed Dating with the Denizens of Underworld

Arachne: Speed Dating with the Denizens of Underworld

Asterion: Speed Dating with the Denizens of Underworld

Hungry Fur Love

Hungry Like Her Wolf: Magic and Mayhem Universe

Hungry For Her Bear: Magic and Mayhem Universe

Shifters Unleashed Boxed Sets

Check out these amazing anthologies where you can find some of my books and the works of other awesome authors!

Midnight Magic Anthology (Water Witch)

Rituals & Runes Anthology (Air Witch)

Island Stripe Pride

Tiger Claimed

Tiger Denied

Tiger Rejected

*Tiger Tales Anthology

NYC Shifter Tales

Cuff Linked

Sealed Fate

A Howlin' Good Fairytale Retelling

Sweet As Candy (single edition coming soon)

<u>Coming Soon:</u>

Hungry As Her Python: Magic and Mayhem Universe

If The Shoe Fits: A Howlin' Good Fairytale Retelling

Chickee and the Paparazzi: FUCN'A

The Wolf's Winter Wish: A Macconwood Pack Tale

The Hybrid Assassin

For Fangs Sake

Tempted By Her Protector: WPU 2

Alien Protector: WPU 3

Elvish Protector: WPU 4

Thrilled By Her Protector: WPU 5

<u>Young Adult Urban Fantasy Books:</u>

Wolf Moon: A Grazi Kelly Novel Book 1

Hunter Moon: A Grazi Kelly Novel Book 2

Rebel Moon: A Grazi Kelly Novel Book 3

Winter Moon: A Grazi Kelly Novel Book 4

Chasing The Moon: A Grazi Kelly Short 5

Blood Moon: A Grazi Kelly Novel 6

*Get all 6 books NOW AVAILABLE IN A BOXED SET:

The Complete Grazi Kelly Novel Series

Casting Magic: The Angela Tanner Files 1

Keeping Magic: The Angela Tanner Files 2

<u>G'Witches Magical Mysteries Series</u>

Co-written with P. Mattern

G'Witches

G'Witches 2: The Harpy Harbinger

G'Witches 3: Summoning Secrets

Excerpt from Wolf Shield: Guardians of Chaos

What a day! Fergie McAndrews headed towards the pick-up truck she'd borrowed from her roommate for work that morning.

Of course, the thirty-thousand dollar certified used luxury car she'd splurged on earlier in the year was in the shop. Again.

Just another in a long line of bad decisions. After leaving a perfectly good job for a startup company, she was laid off three weeks ago and had to borrow money from her parents to pay rent. Wasn't that humiliating?

"This is the last time, Ferg," her step-monster had said after she'd Venmo'd the money to her.

God forbid the mechanic call and tell her the car

was ready. She wouldn't be able to pick it up for another week. That was when she got her first paycheck from her newest gig at L-Corp. Not a startup, but an older company with new offices in Bayonne, which was only a half-hour commute.

But to commute, you needed a car. Fergie had no choice but to borrow the old pick-up from her best friend and roommate, Jessenia Banks. It wasn't like she needed the truck. She worked from home these days. Besides, Fergie promised to fill it up and have it washed.

She huffed out a breath. It'd been a really long day. A crappy one too. Fergie wanted to love her new job. Really, she did. But so far, it was the pits. If Fergie wanted to be a librarian, she would've been one.

Research was her jam. Well, when it was interesting. She had a knack for sniffing out information and compiling easy-to-read spreadsheets and timelines. It wasn't the hard work that annoyed her. Her complaint was the content. The actual stuff her new boss had her looking up. It was beyond boring.

Why an enormous conglomerate like L-Corp needed old land surveys, cross-referenced with newspaper reports on accidents, crimes, etcetera.

She had no idea. She'd been at it for weeks now. So far, she'd researched six locations given via GPS coordinates across Hudson County. Her new boss wanted everything, every little insignificant piece of information she could dig up.

That was the easy part. It was the hassle of the actual job that really made her want to give up. Every day she had to drive to Bayonne to pick up her work laptop she'd dropped off the night before with all of that day's findings. Every single night they wiped her computer clean.

Like she was going to run away with the secrets of what happened on 2nd and Washington sixty-years ago. Can you say paranoid? Ugh.

Fergie had always looked forward to working for a huge global company. It was supposed to be her ticket out of the Garden State. Traveling the globe, seeing new things, visiting far-off places was always a secret dream of hers. Well, that, and having her own walk-in closet full of gorgeous designer shoes.

Best secret dream evah! In her opinion, anyway. What woman didn't love shoes? Fergie hummed as she daydreamed about rows and rows of Blahnik's, Jimmy Choo's, Garavani's, Ferragamo's, and her personal favorites, Louboutin's on every shelf!

Don't judge. Fergie wasn't shallow, she just liked pretty things. Haters gonna hate. But every time she ran across a thrift or second-chance store, she'd search high and low to see what they had. That was how she'd scored the pumps on her feet.

They made her feel good about herself. Being five-foot two-inches short with more curves than a racetrack, Fergie had had more than her fair share of self-esteem issues growing up. Alright, so she was chubby. She could admit that proudly now.

If everyone looked the same, the world would be one boring as hell place. Fergie liked herself perfectly fine these days, in spite of all the times her step-monster tried to make her diet growing up. So she liked food and shoes. Big deal.

She worked hard to feed and clothe herself, so as far as she was concerned, no one had a right to comment. So what if she wanted some excitement in her life? Fergie was aware she was better off than most, but what was wrong with having goals?

She'd spent a lot of time thinking about how a woman like her could have an adventure. Travelling was the only thing she could think of. Of course, she'd been hoping this job would be the answer to that. Even travelling for work was better than being stuck.

Sigh.

So far, her plans had fallen flat, but hey, at least she was earning a paycheck. Her new boss, Mr. Offner, might be a strange man, but he signed her checks, and that was enough for now. Fergie had never seen more than a glimpse of him. All of her instructions usually came via email.

Most of the time she was able to compile her research quickly, then she'd head back to the office to organize it into neat little spreadsheets, and finally, she'd hand it all in with her laptop. But not today.

Mr. Offner sent her an email detailing everything she could dig up on one of the oldest places on record in the county. Of course, land surveys that old, along with police reports, newspaper articles, deeds, and sales records were nowhere she could easily access them.

After wasting hours at both the court house and municipal building, Fergie had been directed to the *second* public library. Apparently anything over a hundred years old was filed away in the godforsaken place. She'd been shocked to find an entire room filled with musty old archives. And wouldn't you know it, there was no cell service and no internet access. Plus, their phone lines were down. She'd had to photograph each page using her cell. When she got home later, she would send those photos like a fax to her boss along with her spreadsheet. If she could manage that before collapsing into bed.

Grab your copy at https://www.cdgorri.com/books/wolf-shield

Excerpt from *Purrfectly Mated*

How the fuck did I wind up here?

It was all Elissa could do not to slam her face down on the table as she pondered that question for the umpteenth time since leaving her cozy Hoboken apartment to go on this so called date.

"So, babe," the over-stuffed, heavily-cologned, and downright fugly man said.

Her date of the evening looked like something out of a bad sitcom as he tried to lean over the stained tablecloth of the rundown hotel buffet room, he'd driven two hours to get to. Waggling his caterpillar-like eyebrows, he gave her the once over and Elissa's skin crawled.

Oh, hell no.

"I got a room upstairs, you know, for *after*," he told her, nodding his head, and biting his lower lip in a manner she assumed he thought was provocative.

At best, it was nauseating.

FML.

How was this guy Elissa's date for the evening? What had she done to deserve this?

Little Gianni. Yup, that was how he'd introduced himself. And here she was. On a blind date with a guy who had the word 'little' in front of his name.

Well, what did she expect? Roses and champagne? In this economy? She didn't know where Cinder-fucking-ella got her prince, but it sure as fuck wasn't in Jersey.

Elissa could only blame herself for agreeing to go on this blind date. Initially, the whole Little Gianni fiasco had been intended for her roommate.

Wait a second. Scratch that thought.

It *was* all Gretchen's fault. That ungrateful cow!

She tried to play it off like she was some sweet little homegrown maiden. Oh, just wait till Elissa got home. Gretchen was never going to hear the end of it.

She owed Elissa. Big time. Like a whole month of

washing the dishes big time. The rat trap they shared in her hometown of Hoboken was all the two women could afford, and for the most part, they got along just fine.

In fact, they'd grown to be close friends over the three years they'd lived together. It was the only reason she'd ever agreed to this date from Hell.

Elissa sighed and looked over at Little Gianni. Maybe he wasn't all that bad?

"*BEEEELLLLLLLLCHHH!* 'Scuse me, doll. Better out, am I right?"

Gianni winked and Elissa wished for a black hole to open up and swallow her up right through the floor.

OMFG.

The man just burped out loud like he was in a frat boy belting contest, only those days passed him up about thirty years ago.

For fuck's sake. Gretchen, you so owe me.

Elissa cursed her roommate and tried not to groan. But Little Gianni wasn't quite done. The grown ass man lifted his leg and let one rip.

Right. Fucking. There.

Elissa was going to die before the end of the night.

Literally.

This is what you get when you do a friend a favor without asking for details! Idiota!

The voice of her Italian grandmother sounded in her brain. She tried to ignore it, willing herself not to wince at the man while he sucked air, and who knows what else, noisily through his coffee-stained teeth.

Ew. So gross.

That was the perfect word to describe it. The only word, in fact. The entire date was just so fucking gross. She still couldn't believe her sweet little roommate from Iowa, *Gretchen Kaepernick*, she of the wispy hair and baby blues, had set her up with this guy!

What the actual fuck was up with that?

Little Gianni was a slob. Actually, he looked just like her Uncle Nico, and that was not a good thing. Seriously, not good at all.

He wore his hair slicked back in a too tight ponytail that emphasized his rapidly receding hairline. As if that wasn't enough to put her off, he was sporting an enormous paunch. Now, being a curvy girl, Elissa appreciated food and was in no way against men showing the same appreciation.

She liked bigger men. Always had. But bigger did not mean you had to be sloppy. Little Gianni's stomach was literally hanging out from under a tight tan golf shirt that had definitely seen better days.

The man didn't even look like he had ever played a sport of any kind. With it, he wore brown polyester pants that were three inches above his ankles and unbuttoned at the waist.

He didn't look like he tried at all for this date. What kind of guy did that? His shirt collar was bent and wrinkled, and all three buttons were open to his chest, revealing a mat of oily, dark hair and pimples.

Somehow, he'd managed to tuck the back of the shirt in, but the front simply would not hold in that stomach. What worried her more were the tight brown pants.

As he sat back and stretched, she wondered if she should take cover. They looked like they were one bite from exploding off his body. Elissa shuddered at the image.

Please God, if You have an ounce of mercy, don't let that happen, she prayed.

"Hang on, doll, I gotta take this," he said, and turned to answer his cell phone.

It was ringing to the tune of '70s disco music she

hadn't heard since the last family reunion. Her eyes kept going to the huge stain on the front of his shirt. It was a little game she liked to call *what the hell is that.*

Coffee, she guessed.

"Up your ass, Bruno. I gotta have it by Monday," he cursed into the receiver.

Elissa winced at the spectacle he was making of them both. There were only a handful of people there, but still.

Deep breaths.

Ew. Maybe not.

She coughed as the strong body spray, that he'd obviously used a ton of in lieu of a shower, bad move in her opinion, invaded her lungs.

Oh, this was so bad.

Elissa was, by no means, a snob. But this guy looked like he'd stepped out of a bad 1980s mafia spoof film. What's worse, he kept smacking his lips together as he hung up the phone and looked her over from head to chest.

Thank fuck for the table, she thought, wishing she could hide her bosoms from his view.

"Ssssss," he hissed, like it was sexy or something.

She just grimaced. Elissa might be able to forgive a lot of quirks, but she hated mouth noises. Really hated them. It was a super pet peeve of hers. Never mind his totally inappropriate and unwelcomed leer.

She started counting the minutes, willing the date to be over already. Plenty of people would tell her she shouldn't be so choosy, but really? She was not this desperate.

Not yet anyway.

So, she was curvy and a little mouthy too. But was it wrong to want a man with good table manners? Even if men were thin on the ground for someone like her.

As a chef, she'd worked in a lot of restaurants and even as a personal cook for professional couples. She'd seen her fair share of unhappy couples and downright uncomfortable marriages. But as far as she was concerned, all relationships went downhill when good table manners were dismissed.

Good manners were merely a sign that a person was thoughtful and respectful. At least, that was what Nonna had told her. Gianni here had clearly missed that lesson as a child. Elissa had to work not to groan in disgust as he slurped a raw clam down his gullet.

Shudder.

Was there no end to his feeding? That's what it reminded her of. Feeding time at the zoo.

OMG. That was rude, she scolded herself. But it wasn't like she said it out loud.

All she wanted to do was go home. At least she was comfortable. *She'd* worn her softest pair of black leggings for this disaster date, paired with one of her favorite tunics on top.

It was dark green with tiny black buttons down the front and showed just the right amount of cleavage. She'd gone for neat and tidy as opposed to downright sexy.

Good call, in her opinion. Elissa looked perfectly fine for a nice *getting to know you* dinner, which is what she thought she was getting when her roommate asked her to step in for her on a blind date that one of her best client's had set up for her.

Elissa shuddered now, thinking how good old Gianni here would've reacted to the red dress and heels she'd contemplated before checking the weather report.

Gulp.

The lewd man was already salivating, and she was so not having it. Fending off his unwanted advances was not how she wanted to finish the night.

Ew again.

Elissa shivered, slightly chilled despite the fact

they were indoors. It was a cold, gloomy evening, and the forecast called for even more rain later that night. Not at all unusual for this time of year in the Garden State.

November was always chilly in the evenings, rainy too. Elissa tended to run warm, but she was glad she'd brought a jacket with her. Especially since her date refused to turn the heat on in the car.

When she'd asked, he'd looked offended and told her it wasted gas.

Um. Okay.

She checked her phone. It was only seven o'clock, but the two hour drive was still ahead of them. Maybe they could make it home before ten if they left soon.

Ugh. Did he just blow his nose?

"Allergies, doll. Say, you gonna eat that?" he asked before scooping a fry from her dish and swallowing it down.

Elissa was gonna kill her roomie. Gretchen was a hair and nail stylist. A lot of her clients were elderly, and they just loved her. They were always offering to set her up on blind dates with their nephews and grandsons.

Mostly, the sweet old ladies were kind. They swore they could find her curvy roommate the right man, assuming she was single because she was new to town. Well, when Elissa got home tonight, she was going to tell Gretchen she needed to fire the old lady who set this date up from being her client.

Like *ASAP*.

No one who liked Gretchen would've sent her out with this guy. Gianni reached over and touched her hand and Elissa pulled back, reaching for the napkin.

Gross.

"I sure hope you ain't a cold one, doll," he said, shaking his head.

"What?"

"Ain't gonna matter. I know just what you need, doll."

She was still wiping the greasy residue he'd transferred to her skin from the food he ate sans utensils. This was too much. Elissa was beyond uncomfortable with all the leering and bad attempts at innuendo.

Plus, she was starving. One look at the dump he'd taken her to, and she knew she could never eat there. The chef in her wouldn't allow it.

To think they drove two hours for this! She'd practically frozen to death in his maroon Cadillac, listening to a CD of the Rat Pack, while Gianni crooned loudly, and off key, to the music.

Normally, she was a fan of the famous group of legendary singers. Having grown up in Hoboken, she couldn't not be a Sinatra fan. Though, to be honest, Dean Martin had always been her favorite.

Still, Elissa was a firm believer that there were just some people you did not try to imitate. Especially not if you were Little Gianni. While he was belting his heart out, he'd been trying to get his right hand on her thigh. She'd asked him politely to stop.

Twice.

Then she'd been forced to try something a little more drastic. Like spilling her hot tea on the offending hand the third time he'd tried it. Finally, he'd removed his hand from her leg. Not making a fourth attempt, which she was grateful for.

Elissa should've taken that behavior as a sign and gotten out of the car. But no. She'd wanted to do Gretchen a solid. So, against her better judgement, she gave the creep another chance.

Idiota, her grandmother's voice echoed in her brain again.

The old woman had loved her. Elissa knew that without a doubt. She'd raised her after her own

parents had passed on in a tragic automobile accident when Elissa was just twelve.

Her grandmother was a no-nonsense kind of
lady who dished out priceless wisdom with brutally
honest insights. It was the same way she dished out
huge bowls of pasta with her amazing meatballs and
homemade sauce. Not to mention a side order of
back-breaking hugs that Elissa still missed.

Nonna cooked like that all the time. She made a
huge pot of sauce every weekend, and she was happy
to serve it to Elissa and her teammates and friends,
especially after games and tournaments.

Soccer had been her sport of choice, and cooking
had soon become her favorite hobby. Her grandmother had encouraged her in both pursuits.
Guiding her in one and cheering her on in the other.
Elissa still missed her terribly.

"Hey babe, ain't you gonna eat nothin'? You know
they charge twenty dollars just to sit down," Little
Gianni interrupted her train of thought.

Elissa was forced to turn her mind back to the
present, which unfortunately included watching, *and
hearing,* him as he sucked on his teeth and stuffed
another breaded shrimp down his throat.

"I'm fine," she answered with a polite smile plastered on her face.

Just get home, Lissa. Just get him to take you home.

Elissa closed her eyes when he looked back down at his dish. Thank God for small favors, she mused. At least he was more interested in eating at the moment.

He'd taken her to the rattiest looking hotel and casino she'd ever seen in her life. And the buffet room?

Ew.

Seriously, the place had to be violating at least a dozen health codes. When Gianni had said Atlantic City, she'd thought at least the atmosphere would be exciting. But they were so far from the real glitz and entertainment, they might as well be anywhere else.

She sighed, looking at the plate she'd made for herself. Elissa couldn't even fake an interest in the food. As a chef, it was hard enough to dine out.

She was always judging the food, the service, the ingredients. How could she not? It was her business. And that was when the food was good!

This was not good. Not at all.

She'd been to hospitals that served better food. Old yellow lights buzzed and blinked around the buffet, giving it an abandoned kind of feel. The menu was made up of mostly frozen then fried or baked cuisine.

Reheated actually. It was like a giant TV dinner buffet where every item was previously frozen when already cooked and warmed up in an oven.

It was the kind of food sold cheap at restaurant supply stores in bulk. Yeah, this was much worse than hospital food, in her opinion.

There was a worn carpet on the floor, a handful of scattered tables in the dining room, elevator music on in the background, and the entire place smelled like canned soup.

Not to mention not one of the five people there besides them was under sixty years old.

"Gianni," she said, leaning forward so as not to hurt his feelings.

"I thought you mentioned something about seeing a show tonight. Is it here?"

Please don't be here.

If he was taking her somewhere else, she could beg off and hire a cab to take her home. There was no way she was sitting through anything else with this man. Not now. Not ever.

"Ah, I see, babe, you want some entertainment first, I get it," he snickered loudly, and she blanched.

Whatever he thought was going to happen wasn't. She needed to disabuse him of the notion, and fast.

"Alright, alright. Lemme finish this, babe. Then we'll go up to the room I got for us," he said.

Before she could make sense of the ludicrous statement, he slurped another fried shrimp, don't ask how. Then he grabbed her arm and yanked her from the seat before she could even react.

Elissa tugged on his hold, but the man was immovable. Tossing a five-dollar bill on the table, Little Gianni snatched a toothpick from the hostess stand before dragging her outside.

Great, he was a cheap tipper, too.

All she wanted was to go home. Figuring the best way to do that would probably be to get him to the car, she let him lead the way.

Once inside, she would ask him to drive back to Hoboken so she could wring Gretchen's neck. Fuming, she pulled her arm out of his hand and walked behind him.

The rain was really pouring, and the cheap bastard had refused valet. Elissa ducked her head so she wouldn't get so wet. Of course, the jacket she'd brought was light and had no hood.

Gianni had an umbrella, but he didn't offer to hold it for her, and honestly, she did not relish the idea of getting any closer to him than necessary.

Seriously, not happening.

Now all she had to do was break the news. She had no intention of watching a show or returning to the hotel with him.

What could go wrong?

Grab your copy at https://www.cdgorri.com/books/purrfectly-mated!

Troy Waman looked down at his smartphone to the little red arrow blinking on his map app, indicating he had reached his destination. He frowned pensively before shaking his head.

"What a fucking shithole," he murmured to himself as he exited the nondescript black SUV his Station Master, Rex, had given him for the job.

"Try not to scratch it," the tough Bear shifter had said with a barely contained growl after their meeting the day before last. After a thousand years of waiting, The *Wardens of Terra* were being called to duty and this was Troy's first assignment.

It took him a day and a half to make his way to Shadowland, New York from the little suburb in Virginia Beach where his Station was located. There were dozens of them across the continental United States and even more overseas, though he'd rarely been out of the county himself.

Troy rolled his shoulders and exhaled. He was the first from his Station to be called to duty. A fact that left him both proud and humbled at the same time. He'd trained damn hard since he was a child waiting for such an opportunity. Now he had it, and it was almost too much to bear.

Fuck and damn. It's time Troy, get your ass in gear. That was all the sympathy he had for himself. Why the hell should he have any at all? Troy Waman was no tenderfoot normal. He was a Warden of Terra. He didn't need to remind himself of the honor and duty that went along with his position.

The *Wardens of Terra* were an ancient group of elite warriors. All of them Shifters. Identified in their youth and trained throughout their preternaturally long lives, they were guardians as well as fighters. *Station Masters* led teams of Wardens across the planet.

Though they'd been deactivated sometime in the last millennium, Wardens were born, chosen, and trained every day with the distinct knowledge that someday, they'd be called upon to defend the earth. That day was here.

Troy Waman had been trained as a Warden since before he learned how to spell the word. His heritage was a mix of Anglo and Native American. His father's blood was a mix of tribes including Algonquin, Lenape, Cherokee, and a few others. He hadn't stuck around long enough for anyone to learn the rest.

He supposed he could get a DNA test, but that might raise too many questions with the normals. Especially in this day of advanced technology in biogenetics.

Besides, it was quite common in today's world to find Native American peoples descended from multiple tribes. Troy Waman was uncommon for an entirely different reason. He was a Shifter, a special race of dual natured beings with one foot in the supernatural world and one in the human. Troy was a *Thunderbird Shifter* to be exact. Something unique even amongst Shifters.

He stretched his long, lithe body as he stepped away from the vehicle. It was already dark out despite it being fairly early in the evening. *Daylight savings my ass.* He sniffed the frigid air. The unusually high winds made the cold seem even more bitter. The street lamp stuttered on the corner, a rusty fence squeaked, and a black cat crossed the street, ducking under some parked cars. Troy's frown deepened.

It looked like the setting of a B-horror flick. All it needed was some half naked co-ed to run down the street with a masked bogeyman stalking behind her, traditional blood-coated knife in hand. *Oh yeah.* They might call it *Shadowland Nightmare* or something equally cheesy.

He stopped his musings and used his heightened senses to take in the downtrodden area around him. It would seem upstate New York wasn't all orchards and sprawling suburbs. He smirked as the "I love New York" song ran through his head. *Yeah, right.*

Apparently, parts of the Empire State were as fucked up as the street where he was born in Newark, New Jersey. He'd visited that shithole back when he was in his teens just out of curiosity. What a mistake that had been! He'd left almost as soon as he'd arrived. His extended family had been, shall we say, less than welcoming.

His gray-haired grandmother had screamed and crossed herself when he stepped over her threshold. He was what they called a *skin walker*. They feared and loathed him as something evil. Him evil? Like he was the motherfucker who knocked-up some unsuspecting normal and left her ass with a Shifter baby.

He was not evil, but he was something they did not understand. He'd been angry and ashamed that day. He'd crashed through his grandmother's kitchen to hitch a ride back down to his Station in Virginia Beach.

In his youth it was more like a military training camp, but it was all he knew of home. After all, it was where he'd lived his entire life. He'd made his peace and settled fully into his life there.

The incident with his grandmother had happened over a decade ago, when Troy had stolen his records out of Rex's office. Still, the memory remained fresh in his mind as if it were only yesterday. The fucked-up street where he was standing only brought back the painful reminder that he'd come from the same kind of squalor. *Fuck this*, he thought.

The pungent scent of despair washed over him. *Reminding him.* A young man with a hood pulled up over his head, eyed him from the street corner. *Drug dealer. Shadowland* indeed. It was an apt name for this shamble of a neighborhood.

The young man continued to stare until Troy allowed his beast to shine through. His golden eyes pinned the errant youth through the inky darkness of the night. Startled, the kid dropped the bag he was holding and ran down the alley.

Punk. Troy walked over and picked up what he had so hastily left behind. A couple of grams of crack cocaine and heroin, *probably cut with Fentanyl.* There were also various sized baggies full of what smelled like some below average marijuana and half-rotted psychedelic mushrooms.

Just your garden variety of illegal substances to be found on most street corners in neighborhoods like this one. *Fucking normals.* He frowned and dumped the still sealed contents down the closest storm drain. He sent a quick text to Rex earmarking the location.

Rex would make sure the local police department got an anonymous tip to retrieve the narcotics before someone got hurt. Recreational drug use, mainly the opioid epidemic, was wreaking havoc amongst the humans with more and more of them succumbing to their addictions.

It was troubling, but not Troy's problem. Shifters were extraordinarily hard to kill. Most human drugs had little to no effect on supernatural beings. *Normals,* he growled the thought, *such weak creatures.*

To be fair, Shifters had vices too. He just had little

experience with it. Cecil, a Station-mate of his, had an adrenaline addiction. He was always putting himself in dangerous situations, even during simple training exercises. Fernandez, a Jaguar Shifter, was always trying to get into some chick's pants. *Sex addict.* And he knew of others who channeled their energies into ways he considered to be mostly unproductive.

His opinion, for sure. He'd always been something of a loner by nature. There weren't many Thunderbird Shifters around. Hell, he was the only fucking one he knew of in this part of the world.

He didn't blame or judge his Station-mates for their proclivities. Most of the Shifters he knew had large appetites which included food, exercise, and sex.

Troy had certainly explored that part of him. He wasn't a man-whore or anything, but he'd had his share of women. None of them mattered to him. Just a means to satisfy the occasional itch.

Troy was determined to live his life as a Warden of Terra alone. He never expected to find anyone willing to share what was a potentially deadly existence.

Those who followed the Darkness and evil were always looking for ways to gain the upper hand and it was his job to stop them. The way he saw it, it was an honor and a duty to serve.

He shared this great responsibility with the entire organization. The core belief of the Wardens was based on one indisputable fact Shifters had walked the earth since the dawn of time, even before humankind; therefore, they were responsible for the well-being of the entire planet and all its inhabitants. Especially those who were inherently weaker. Mainly females and *normals*.

There were other supernaturals who believed humans, or normals as they referred to them, were a blight on the planet. Those creatures wished to destroy them and take over.

Demons, Dark Witches, and a whole plethora of evil beings sought the destruction of the normals and the world they lived in. *Idiots! Did they even realize if they destroyed the world, there would be nothing left? Where the fuck would they live?*

Of course, the supernatural world had many agencies that worked towards the common goal of saving the planet. The *Order of the Guardians*, for example, were responsible for policing the various factions of supernaturals.

Shifters generally tended to ally themselves with the Guardians. Sure, there were *bad* Shifters, but he'd never come across any willing to follow the Dark. Simply because most agreed the destruction of the world could not be allowed to happen.

Different Packs and Clans, etcetera, of course, had different ideas. Some wanted to remain secret, others wished to come out, and other still wanted to rule the weaker humans. It was a whole fucking thing, and they argued about regularly.

Troy didn't know from any of that. He spent little time in the human world. His efforts better spent making himself worthy of being a Warden. Training, exercise, and following orders. That's what Troy lived for, it was why he was chosen.

Thunderbird Shifters were very rare. *Special.* He scoffed at the stray thought. But no matter what way he looked at it, Troy was indeed unique. In more ways than one. He was born *marked* by the stars. A *Shifter of Terra.*

From infancy, he was told he carried the power of his sign within him. *Aquarius* ruled his destiny and it would aid him in the never-ending battle against the forces of darkness.

Every single Warden he knew was a Shifter like him. They were the fiercest warriors on the planet. Like many others throughout the last thousand years, Troy, *a Shifter child who was marked,* was taken from his parents and trained by his Station Master until the time when he would be called into use.

All that time, he thought, *and here I am.* He tried to ignore the pressure building inside of him. He felt anxious. His animal pressed against his psyche, comforting him with his presence.

The significance of the moment was not lost on him. The Wardens had waited a millennium to be called to act. *He* had been waiting his entire life.

"Do not fear the future, Troy," the Herald who had visited his Station said to him when he'd brought word that they had been activated, *"Your destiny awaits."*

Troy wondered if the old man referred to the Wardens finally being called to act, or if the elder spoke of yet another legend. Troy had been shocked to say the least when the Herald had entered their tidy little Station in Virginia Beach with his flowing white hair. After he told them the news, he turned to Troy and recited another old tale.

"Young Thunderbird, you are the first to return us to Terra. Do not doubt your worth. Your destiny has been written in the stars since before you were born, Troy Waman. Remember, a Warden discovers his true measure when his fated mate is thrust upon him."

Whatever the fuck that meant. Troy looked down at

his phone, then to the street sign on the corner, and finally, to the faded numbers painted on the mailbox in front of the ramble of a house his map app had brought him to.

Fuck, am I thinking? Fated mates are myths. Stories made up so orphaned Shifters would sleep through the night. He scoffed at the thought. Memories of tales the head nurse, Sr. Maria, had told him at the training camp he'd called home for years invaded his brain.

Memories were pesky things. Sometimes eternal, and always fucking portable. But he was no longer a child. *No more stories, Sister. Now, I act.*

"A thousand years we've waited, and I'm walking into a fucking scene from a bad episode of *Hoarders*," Troy shook his head and frowned at the decrepit house that sat a few hundred feet away from him.

It was cold as fuck outside and his leather jacket did little to warm him. Avian Shifters did not carry around the same bulk as other types of Shifters. He ran hotter than normals, but the single digit temperature froze him to the bone.

True, he wasn't beefy like some of his fellow Shifters, but he was just as incredibly strong, and he was wicked fast. Much stronger than any average male. He paused briefly gauging the atmosphere.

There was something off about the place. He scented *Magic* and something else. His Bird bristled beneath his skin. *Easy now.*

Lightning flashed in the darkened skies, allowing him to see the worn shingles, and cracked siding of the beaten-up colonial in greater detail. More than one window had been smashed and boarded up with cheap plywood.

If anything, it enhanced the creepy haunted house feel of the place. The porch sagged danger-ously. He wondered how the place had managed to not be condemned by the town. One thing was certain, it was an ugly little turd of a house.

Who the hell put gray siding on their house anyway? Maybe it wasn't always that color. Maybe the owner liked gray. *Whatever.* He couldn't give two shits about the siding.

His only concern was the increased supernatural activity in the area over the past two weeks. Ever since the owner, a *Mrs. Renalda Curosi,* passed away. *A haunting?*

A creaking sound floated up to his ears and he stilled his movements. The sound developed into more of a *moaning* noise. An unearthly wail. It grew louder as the lightning continued to flash in the sky.

Troy had never seen a ghost. True, there were a

lot of things in the universe he had never seen nor heard of, but that didn't make them any less real.

If ghosts were real, and they made noises, he imagined that pitiful wail was damn close to what it would sound like.

No such thing as ghosts. Yeah, well, most people had never heard of Shifters either. And yet, there he stood.

His Thunderbird shifted once more beneath his skin, the beast flexing his senses as the lightning in the air drew him to the surface. *No.* He told his other half. His human needed to be in control now. He walked across the street, keeping to the shadows.

Something was indeed off about the creepy old house. He inched further to the black door. The knocker was in the shape of a face or mask. No discernible features, just a vague impression of eyes, nose, and mouth. *Shadowland indeed.*

He listened with his enhanced hearing and frowned. There was a distinct voice somewhere beneath the moaning and creaking. A *female* voice. His curiosity was piqued.

From what he'd seen in her file, Mrs. Curosi was ninety-seven when she passed. Her closest living relative was a half-sister, a *Magdelena Kristos,* and she lived over three hours away in New Jersey. The half-sister was cut from Mrs. Curosi's will recently. She'd bequeathed her entire estate, house, bank account, and all her earthly belongings, to someone named *A. Kristos. Another sister? Maybe.*

Troy hadn't given it much thought until now. A crash sounded from inside the house. He perked up as the feminine voice he'd thought he'd heard earlier screamed in pain. *Time to act.*

Grab your copy at https://www.cdgorri.com/books/bound-by-airbooks/bound-by-air!

About the Author

C.D. Gorri is a USA Today Bestselling author of steamy paranormal romance and urban fantasy. She is the creator of the Grazi Kelly Universe.

Join her mailing list here: https://www.cdgorri.com/newsletter

An avid reader with a profound love for books and literature, when she is not writing or taking care of her family, she can usually be found with a book or tablet in hand. C.D. lives in her home state of New Jersey where many of her characters or stories are based. Her tales are fast paced yet detailed with satisfying conclusions.

If you enjoy powerful heroines and loyal heroes who face relatable problems in supernatural settings, journey into the Grazi Kelly Universe today. You will find sassy, curvy heroines and sexy, love-driven heroes who find their HEAs between the pages. Werewolves, Bears, Dragons, Tigers, Witches, Romani, Lynxes, Foxes, Thunderbirds, Vampires, and many more Shifters and supernatural creatures dwell within her worlds. The most important thing is every mate in this universe is fated, loyal, and true lovers always get their happily ever afters.

Want to know how it all began? Enter the Grazi Kelly Universe with Wolf Moon: A Grazi Kelly Novel or pick up Charley's Christmas Wolf and dive into the Macconwood Pack Novel Series today.

For a complete list of C.D. Gorri's books visit her website here:

https://www.cdgorri.com/complete-book-list/

Thank you and happy reading!

del mare alla stella,
   C.D. Gorri

Follow C.D. Gorri here:
   http://www.cdgorri.com

https://www.facebook.com/Cdgorribooks
https://www.bookbub.com/authors/c-d-gorri
https://twitter.com/cgor22
https://instagram.com/cdgorri/
https://www.goodreads.com/cdgorri
https://www.tiktok.com/@cdgorriauthor